Wallace
Box 15
Coral, PA
15731

Comforting Arms

Virginia Jacober
Psalm 23:1

Virginia Jacober

Copyright © 2006 by Virginia Jacober

All rights reserved. No part of this book shall be reproduced or transmitted in any form or by any means, electronic, mechanical, magnetic, photographic including photocopying, recording or by any information storage and retrieval system, without prior written permission of the publisher. No patent liability is assumed with respect to the use of the information contained herein. Although every precaution has been taken in the preparation of this book, the publisher and author assume no responsibility for errors or omissions. Neither is any liability assumed for damages resulting from the use of the information contained herein.

This is a work of fiction. Names, characters, places, and incidents either are the product of the author's imagination or are used fictitiously. Any resemblance to actual events or locales or persons, living or dead, is entirely coincidental.

ISBN 0-7414-2999-3

All Scripture quotations are taken from the Holy Bible, King James Version.

Published by:

1094 New DeHaven Street, Suite 100
West Conshohocken, PA 19428-2713
Info@buybooksontheweb.com
www.buybooksontheweb.com
Toll-free (877) BUY BOOK
Local Phone (610) 941-9999
Fax (610) 941-9959

Printed in the United States of America
Printed on Recycled Paper
Published January 2006

Acknowledgments

With deep and lasting gratitude I thank my talented Sunday School teacher and valued friend, Woodie Style, who graciously and generously shared his time and skill by putting this manuscript on his computer, arranged the detailed format and offered wise technical as well as editorial advice.

I also appreciate the time-consuming work of Woodie's granddaughter, Barbara Vivlamore, for her kindness in professionally editing the manuscript.

My prayer partner, Marge Whiteman, deserves my heartfelt thanks for her truly encouraging phone calls and faithful, specific intercession to our Heavenly Father on my behalf.

*This book is dedicated to all who love
The Holy Land
and the people who live there.*

Comforting Arms

Contents

1. The Valley of Blessing - Berachah — 1
2. The Judean Mountains — 8
3. Bethlehem — 14
4. The Fields of Boaz — 22
5. Old Beersheba — 29
6. New Beersheba — 37
7. In a Bedouin Tent — 47
8. The Wilderness of Paran — 57
9. The Red Sea — 66
10. Solomon's Bay — 73
11. Mt. Sinai — 80
12. Joppa — 89
13. Caesarea — 94
14. Mt. Carmel — 100
15. Nazareth — 107
16. Galilee — 115
17. Gaza — 124
18. Jericho — 133
19. Massada — 141
20. Jerusalem — 150
21. The Old City Gates — 159
22. Ein Karim — 170
23. Bethany and the Mount of Olives — 178
24. Easter — 186

Chapter 1

The Valley of Blessing - Berachah

Abby had warned her friends that security in the Holy Land would be tight. They had nodded and assumed they understood. Their first surprise came when they boarded the plane in Atlanta. On each seat lay a notice from KLM, the Royal Dutch Airlines. It was headlined,

> INFORMATION TO PASSENGERS WITH
> DESTINATION TEL AVIV

Dear Passenger,

Although your luggage is labeled through to Tel Aviv, it is important for you to know that it will be unloaded at Amsterdam Airport where its contents will be checked for security reasons prior to departure for Tel Aviv.

You will be requested to identify personally your baggage in the designated area next to the departure gate.

Baggage control is possible as from 3 hours until 45 minutes before departure.

In order to prevent that your bags cannot be checked due to lack of time and, as a consequence, are left behind, you are kindly requested to proceed for their identification at the earliest possible time.

Abby read the notice and quietly assured her group that there was nothing to worry about. Five friends from her church had asked her to take them on a private tour. She was a missionary who had lived in Bethlehem for eighteen years.

With her knowledge of the country, she could easily plan a practical and informative daily program.

"I don't like the idea of anyone searching my luggage," complained Lisa, the youngest member of the tour. "Why didn't you tell us about this, Abby?"

"It's a new regulation, Lisa. This is the first I've known about it. But please don't worry. They look for explosives or firearms. It's a routine investigation to ensure your safety. The fighting between the Jews and the Arabs has escalated, and there is stringent security as a result."

The travelers slept fitfully during the overnight flight to Holland. After checking their luggage, the customs official asked for their cameras. One by one, with their permission, he snapped each owner's picture. Lisa frowned until the handsome official smiled at her. She instantly melted and handed him her camera, then posed gracefully.

Their next culture shock came en route to Israel that morning.

"Who are those men standing at the back of the plane? They're dressed in black. Are they terrorists getting ready to skyjack us?" Megan asked in a frightened whisper. "Look, they're swaying back and forth. That's strange behavior."

"And they're mumbling something unintelligible," added her husband, Colin.

"No, they're not terrorists. They're religious Jews chanting prayers," Abby answered. "You'll see a variety of people, customs and places in the Holy Land."

Some of the passengers shouted and cheered as the plane landed in Tel Aviv.

"Why are they doing that?" Lisa scowled. Megan wanted to ask the same question. She was glad the tall, beautiful blonde had done it for her.

"The Jewish people are glad to be back in Israel. They believe it is their homeland," Abby replied.

Colin watched a few of the travelers kneel and kiss the ground. "It looks like they really are happy to be here,"

The Valley of Blessing – Berachah

he murmured, "and I am, too."

"This is going to be a unique vacation," remarked Andrew, a fourth member of the group, as they walked into the airport.

"I agree," said his wife, Cindy. "I'm glad we came. And I'm glad I rolled my hair into a French twist. It's quite warm here for springtime."

After they retrieved their luggage and passed through customs, Abby led her team outside to a van. The driver rushed them along the main highway toward Jerusalem.

"What are all those funny black posts standing like little soldiers lined up in the fields?" Megan asked. "Colin says I ask too many questions, but I'm curious."

"Those are grapevine stumps," explained Abby. "Soon the leaves will begin to sprout. Look! Those stone buildings perched in the mountains up ahead are our first glimpse of Jerusalem."

In the Holy City, they wound along streets packed with cars, buses, trucks, taxis, people and donkeys carrying loads.

"It's filled with traffic like our cities at home," remarked Cindy, "but we don't have donkeys on our streets! And some of the people look different."

"There are Jewish immigrants from many countries of the world, plus Arabs and lots of tourists. They use three main languages," Abby explained. "The Jews speak Hebrew, the Arabs Arabic and a lot of the people know English."

"Why are there so many soldiers everywhere? It's frightening!" Lisa's voice shook.

"Well," Abby replied, "ever since terrorism increased a few years ago, more Israeli soldiers are posted to guard strategic roads. When you enter some of the buildings in Jerusalem, you must open your purse and any bag you carry, for inspection at the door."

"I suppose it's a safety precaution," Andrew commented, shifting his long legs into a more comfortable position and smoothing back his straight black hair.

3

"Exactly. Occasionally someone smuggles in a bomb timed to explode."

"Oh no! If I had known this trip would be that dangerous, I never would have come. Why didn't you tell us?" Lisa turned to face Abby, her big blue eyes wide with fear.

"If you remember, at our orientation meeting I did explain about Jewish-Arab animosity. But I believe we are not in any danger, and we will plan to go only to places where it is safe. God is our Protector. Nothing can harm us that He does not permit."

"The buildings all look like they are made of stone," observed Colin, changing the subject. He was a highly successful civil engineer. "When something involves my profession, I'm as curious as my wife!"

"It's a government rule that every building must be faced with stone. There are literally mountains of it in Judea. Most of the new buildings are cement block faced with a veneer of stone. But the old houses were made of extremely thick stone, some of them three feet wide. They stay cool in summer, but unfortunately they are like blocks of ice in winter!"

In a high-pitched voice, Lisa asked, "But surely the hotels are heated?"

"Yes, modern buildings have central heating. But many private homeowners use little kerosene heaters they carry from room to room. Electric ones are available, but purchasing and operating them is extremely expensive. At Christmas time the people roast chestnuts on top of their small heaters, and they place orange peel or incense on it to make the house smell fragrant."

"Well, it's a good thing we're here when the weather is warm," Lisa decided. "I hope there is air conditioning?"

"In some hotels, yes. But not where we are staying. The weather does cool down at night, though, because we're in the Judean mountains. You might even need a light blanket. Buildings retain the coolness most of the day, and

The Valley of Blessing – Berachah

it's surprisingly like natural air conditioning."

"Oh. Then there must be fans? I won't be able to sleep without one."

"Yes. We'll make sure your room is comfortable."

In a large parking lot filled with cars, trucks and taxis, the group transferred, along with their luggage, to another van that took them fifteen miles farther south, past vineyards, fields and villages to a valley lush with pine and fruit trees. They stopped in front of a large, rambling, neat building surrounded by flowers and low stone walls.

"We're staying in this guest home managed by a personal friend of mine."

A caretaker opened the iron gate. Julia Evans, the attractive middle-aged Welsh hostess, welcomed them graciously. In an elegantly furnished lounge she served tea while Abby introduced her friends. "This is Colin Hunter, and Megan his wife. They manage their own construction business. And we brought a medical team with us: Andrew Olsen is a surgeon and his wife, Cindy, is a nurse. Lisa Livingston teaches school."

Julia directed the couples to tastefully decorated private rooms and baths. Without waiting to be assigned a place, Lisa quickly scanned the remaining rooms.

"I'll have this one," she insisted, choosing a comfortable single one for herself, and she promptly plopped her luggage onto the bed.

With raised eyebrows Julia looked at Abby, who slowly shook her head to imply, "That's all right. I don't mind." Julia understood; she didn't tell Lisa that the room she had chosen was always reserved for the tour guide. Abby quickly climbed to the second floor. It was quiet and private because the other rooms were unoccupied. She was content. She had learned long ago to be flexible in any situation and, though it was not always easy, to accept cheerfully whatever came along as from God's hand.

The travel-weary guests were relieved to unpack, shower and enjoy a leisurely dinner, followed by brief

Comforting Arms

devotions in the lounge. Abby read the story of how King Jehoshaphat brought his army to this same valley to celebrate God's miraculous victory over their enemies."'...fear not, nor be dismayed;...for the Lord will be with you.' is the promise God gave to Israel. It's a good one for us, too. The name of this valley is Berachah. It means 'blessing.'

"Today this is still a 'valley of blessing' because it yields bountiful crops of delicious fruit--apples, plums, figs, grapes, apricots--plus a variety of vegetables. Julia preserves the excess produce, and we'll probably get to sample some of it while we're here."

Abby thanked God for a safe journey and said, "Now for a good night's rest. Breakfast is at eight. Pleasant dreams, everyone."

Julia was waiting for Abby in her office, and together they discussed the details of the schedule for the next few days. They were good friends. Abby's grandmother was Welsh, which united the two in a common bond. Julia was medium in height and average in build. Abby was slim and petite. But they both had brown eyes and their hair waved naturally. Their birthdays were in the same year, only a few days apart, and they often celebrated together. A study of family history revealed that they were unrelated but people often mistook them for sisters.

"I must warn you that the fighting has escalated, but my driver will be careful to take you only to places that are safe. We don't want to alarm your friends. Occasionally Jewish soldiers come to inquire about my guests. Sometimes they check passports to make sure no terrorists are hiding here."

"Andrew and Cindy seem calm and capable of adjusting to any situation," Abby replied. "They are in their late thirties. Colin and Megan are slightly younger but they're cheerful and flexible. Their two young children are staying with an aunt for these three weeks. Lisa appears rather fearful and easily upset. I'm afraid she didn't take seriously my warning about conditions here. She's young, only twenty-three, so I'll try to protect her from any unpleasant situation."

"That may not be as easy as you think." Julia frowned. "You're going to have problems with that one. I know from experience. She's a typical troublemaker. There's often one in a group. You have my sympathy and my prayers! Good night now."

Chapter 2

The Judean Mountains

The next morning at breakfast Julia introduced a visitor to the group. "This is Peter, my brother. He arrived late last night."

Abby noticed that his brown hair was beginning to turn slightly gray, as was hers. She judged him to be near her own age, probably in his late forties. He stood tall and straight.

Smiling cheerfully, he asked, "May I join your tour?" His deep voice was rich with a delightful Welsh accent. "I hope Julia will forgive my childhood pranks, and give me a good recommendation."

"You were always the mischievous ringleader when we were growing up, but you're forgiven," she laughed as she gave him a hug. He put his arm around her, and she turned to her guests. "Peter is a seminary professor. His heavy schedule has always prohibited time for sightseeing, but at last he's on extended holiday. I think you Americans call it 'spring break.'"

Abby smiled. "Of course. We'll be happy to have you with us. That will make seven of us in the van we are renting. We share expenses."

Before Peter could express his appreciation, Lisa questioned, "Seven in our van? We were squeezed into the one we came in yesterday."

"No problem, Lisa. Many of them carry more than seven. Our luggage took up a lot of room. Here comes our driver, Samir. We call him Sam. He's a Christian Arab from

The Judean Mountains

a nearby village. Now he lives here, and he works for Julia in the garden and the guest home."

"I'll have the front seat. I want to see everything," Lisa announced firmly as they climbed aboard. She scrambled into the coveted place and deposited her purse and camera beside Sam.

Again, Abby exercised restraint and patience. She did not embarrass her guest by explaining that the front was reserved for the tour guide, and quietly slid into a seat beside Andrew and Cindy in the middle. Colin, Megan and Peter settled in the back.

"Where are we going today?" asked Megan, pushing back an unruly red curl that kept springing in front of her eyes.

Abby smiled. "It's only ten miles from here. Can you guess? I'll give you a hint. It's the little town where the boy David grew up."

Quickly Cindy answered, "Bethlehem!" She had learned Bible stories by heart when she was a child.

"Right. We'll soon be there," Abby assured them. She pointed to one side of the road. "That valley is filled with staked grapevines."

"What's wrong with the other side? It looks like those stumps are fallen over and they're dead. What a shame!" exclaimed Megan.

"It looks that way, but they're very much alive. The old custom is to train each vine to lay prone, resting on a large rock for support, so it won't touch the ground. Either method seems to be effective because they produce huge, sweet, delicious grapes."

"When?" asked Megan.

"Usually beginning in August and lasting through October. I'm sorry we won't get to sample any while we're here. But the monks in a monastery outside Jerusalem bottle delicious grape juice and we can buy some to enjoy."

They swerved a bit too fast around a sharp curve in the smooth, winding mountain road.

"Stop! Stop!" Lisa clapped her hand over her mouth. Sam pulled to one side, and she jumped out quickly. She lost her breakfast and her pride at the same time.

"I've never been carsick before," she muttered. "It's terribly humiliating."

"Think nothing of it. Many people have this problem because of all the curves in these mountain roads. Sam will drive more slowly. Perhaps this will help." Abby handed her a bottle of water and a packet of tissues.

"Since we've stopped here, let's walk down this path past the ruins of that old Turkish fort to Solomon's Pools. We're told that he dug these huge reservoirs to catch the rainwater that poured down the sides of the surrounding mountains. There are three, each one with an overflow system leading into the next. They supplied the water for Jerusalem via aqueduct."

"What a feat of engineering that must have been! I'm impressed. Solomon certainly used the gift of wisdom the Lord gave him," Colin remarked.

"It's a beautiful spot, isn't it, with these luxurious pine trees offering cool shady places for a picnic. Over there are the remains of an aqueduct that still channels water down the mountain. During the winter rains, all three pools collect a bit of water, but most of it fills this first one."

"We don't read about this in the Bible, do we?" asked Andrew.

"Some scholars think Solomon's words, 'I made me pools of water,' refers to these. We know he cultivated gardens and orchards that would have needed watering. This could have been the source of his supply. There are still productive gardens beyond these pools.

"Let's go on now. This may be the same road the Wise Men traveled when they followed the star in search of the King."

As they neared Bethlehem, Abby asked, "Do you remember the gifts they brought to Jesus?"

"Gold, incense and..." Megan hesitated.

The Judean Mountains

"Myrrh," added Colin. "But I've often wondered why? There must be some significance. I didn't go to Sunday School or church when I was a child, and I have a lot to catch up on."

"Peter, would you like to explain?" Abby asked.

"I'll be happy to. Perhaps Mary and Joseph needed those costly gifts to sell so they could use the money to live on when they fled to Egypt. Gold represents divinity. Jesus was God in the form of a man. Incense is an aromatic compound that exudes its aroma when it is burned, like the Christians' prayers that smell sweet and fragrant before God's throne. Myrrh is the resin of a tree that grows in the East. It was used as a perfume for embalming, and reminds us of Jesus' death."

"Thanks, Peter," Colin said. "Now I understand."

"Why are we stopping, and what are those soldiers going to do?" asked Lisa shakily.

"This is an Israeli military checkpoint. I hope you all have your passports handy because we will need to show them," Abby said.

"I don't like this. I don't like it at all," Lisa complained. However, when a young, good-looking soldier looked into the van and glanced at her, she instantly smiled and cooperated.

"We're on a private tour of the Holy Land," Abby explained.

The soldier scrutinized each passport, checked the pictures with each person, then gave them back and waved the travelers on.

"We're passing Rachel's Tomb." Abby pointed to a low, domed cement building beside the road. "Jacob buried her where she died. Now Israeli women go there to pray for a child because they believe Rachel prays for the children of Israel. They consider it one of their most sacred shrines. That high wall surrounds it for protection, and soldiers guard the entrance because of the danger posed by terrorists who look for opportunities to destroy their enemies.

"Here's another question for you. It sounds simple but

many people do not know what the place might have looked like. Where was Jesus born?"

"In a stable."

"Right. What kind of stable was it?"

"Like a barn," spoke up Colin.

"Right again. But what kind of barn?"

"Like my father's barn on his farm back home," Andrew answered.

"What is it made of?"

"Wood."

"There probably are no barns like that in the Holy Land. Wood is very expensive. The Israeli government has a re-forestation program called 'Plant a Tree,' and you can participate. They dig the holes and provide the young trees. All you do is put it in the hole and cover it with dirt. And, you pay for the privilege!"

"I wondered why some of these mountains look bare and stony," Megan said.

"Until the British came in 1918, the Turks ruled the country and taxed the trees. To avoid paying, the owners cut them down. As a result, erosion took place, stripping the mountains bare. Now the much-needed forests are being replaced.

"Tell me, where do you think the manger might have been?"

"In a house?" Cindy suggested. "In some countries people keep livestock in the house for warmth or safety."

"Under a house built on stilts?" Colin guessed.

Lisa snickered. "In this country? No way."

"Actually, Colin, that's a good guess," Abby answered. "I've seen what you described in a village. Now here we are in Bethlehem."

Sam parked the van and they began to climb an asphalt road up a short, steep hill. Lisa stopped halfway and looked helplessly at Peter. "I need some assistance," she begged, gasping for breath. He graciously offered her his arm.

Abby noticed Lisa's smug expression and began to wonder about her motive. Was she actually that helpless? True, she was beautiful, and she dressed elegantly in the latest fashions to emphasize her lovely eyes, hair and figure. But did her heart match her outward appearance? That question remained to be answered. She seemed rather self-centered and inconsiderate of others. So far, her behavior left much to be desired.

Chapter 3

Bethlehem

The steep hill opened out into a flat area. "This is the center of Bethlehem, called 'Manger Square,'" Abby explained to her friends. "It's surrounded by shops, a mosque, a church and a police station.

"Notice that large star on the roof of the church. It shines so brightly at night you can see it from a long distance away. It reminds us that Jesus is the 'light of the world.' My husband said the five points on the Arab star stand for the five names of Jesus: Wonderful, Counselor, Mighty God, Everlasting Father and Prince of Peace."

"But the Jewish star has six points," Andrew said. "Do they represent anything?"

"Yes," Abby answered, "John believed the triangle pointing upward was a spiritual picture: one side represented God the Father, one the Son and the other is the Holy Spirit, the Trinity. The triangle pointing down showed humanity: man's body, soul and spirit. The triangles of God and man are intertwined and cannot be separated."

"I haven't heard that before," Peter said. "I'm impressed. Your husband?"

"He was a minister in the church, loved by the Jerusalem congregation. He died six years ago."

"I'm sorry. I've been through that grief. My wife died four years ago. It takes time for the healing process. You draw closer to the Lord and depend upon Him for comfort. Yet there is always that emptiness, that loneliness."

"Yes. Thank you, Peter. You do understand. I'm sorry about your loss. It helps to keep busy. I returned here for another four-year term of missionary work. During furloughs I traveled extensively to speak in churches about missions. But you're quite right, there is always the feeling that half of you is missing."

Turning to the group, Abby said, "Here in Manger Square on the morning of Christmas Eve, Arab Boy and Girl Scout Troops from all parts of the Holy Land parade with flags, drums and trumpets. In the evening, choirs from many countries of the world come to sing carols and celebrate the birth of Jesus. At midnight all of the churches in Bethlehem ring their bells in honor of Christmas Day.

"Jewish soldiers patrol in jeeps to make sure no terrorists play havoc during the celebrations. A few years ago a bomb did go off nearby, and instantly, soldiers sprang up the walls to find the perpetrator. Now let's go into that big stone church. It's managed by the Greek Orthodox priests. Originally the wooden roof was covered with lead but when the Muslims ruled, they used the lead to make bullets."

"But there's only a tiny door. How can we?" Lisa saw people stooping to get through it. "I refuse to be so humiliated. Once today is enough."

"Why is it so little?" asked Megan, pushing back the unruly red curl that insisted on creeping over her left eye.

"The Turks ruled the land for four hundred years. They were Muslims, who do not believe Jesus was God in human form, and that He died on the cross. They say Christians are heretics. So they threatened to ride their horses into the church and trash it. To prevent this from happening, that arch above the door was filled in with more stones. It's a good way to humble us as we bend down to enter the building. Let's go in now."

In spite of her protests, Lisa condescended to go along. They passed huge marble pillars and ancient icons picturing Bible characters: Moses, Elisha, John and Mary. Artistic mosaics lay beneath open squares of the wooden floor. Lamps and candles burned with a soft glow. The fragrance of incense permeated the air.

Steps led down to a small, dark room. Lisa grabbed Peter's hand for support. The walls of stone were blackened by smoke from more lamps and candles.

"Oh, now I see!" exclaimed Cindy. "Jesus was born in a cave!"

"Right," Abby said. "Shepherds still keep their sheep and goats in caves in these Judean mountains. They're warm in winter and cool in summer, so they make ideal stables."

She pointed to a big silver star set into the marble floor. "This marks the spot where people believe Jesus was born. These places where Bible stories occurred are sacred to Christians from all over the world. Churches were built over the sites for protection from enemies who attempted to destroy them. Think of what happened here long ago and how much it means to us."

Abby led the way through a passage to the adjacent Catholic Church. "Let's sit down in this little chapel and sing a Christmas carol. Here are the words to 'O Little Town of Bethlehem.'" She handed each of them a card. "Notice the third verse:"

'How silently, how silently,
The wondrous gift is giv'n!
So God imparts to human hearts
The blessing of His heav'n.
No ear may hear His coming,
But in this world of sin,
Where meek souls will receive Him still,
The dear Christ enters in.'

Following a brief time of silent meditation, they climbed back up the steps and walked quietly out of the church.

"The people of Bethlehem are all Arabs. Most of them are Christians from a Greek Orthodox, Roman Catholic or Lutheran background. Some Muslims have moved in because Christians have sold them land and emigrated to safer countries. There are no Jews living here."

"Why?" asked Megan. "I know I'm always asking why. There goes my insatiable curiosity again. Forgive me for being so inquisitive."

"There's nothing to forgive. You're here to learn, and I'll be happy to answer as many of your questions as I can.

"Actually, Jordan has a law that if an Arab in the West Bank sells land to a Jew, he can't return to his roots in Jordan, or he will be executed. Previously, Palestinian Arabs used to travel freely back and forth from the West Bank to Jordan, to visit their relatives. Now there are Israeli restrictions, with lengthy body and luggage searches at the bridge between the two countries. Travelers wait for hours in the heat for their turn, and sometimes they're turned away or told to come back the next day. Upon their return from Jordan, they face humiliating procedures by customs officials who have been known to rip open the shoulder pads of men's suits, or to pull the heels off women's shoes in their search for hidden weapons or explosive devices.

"Also, this is Jesus' birthplace. Most Jews don't believe He is the Messiah, and they don't accept the New Testament as God's Word. Perhaps this is why they prefer not to live here. Another reason is that it would be extremely risky. There is too much animosity between the Jews and Arabs for them to live harmoniously in such close proximity.

"Sporadic riots in the city of Hebron proved this point. Jews moved into Muslim neighborhoods, and violence resulted. They felt it was their right to live there, and they wanted to prove it.

"They have taken over Arab land a few miles south of here, built their own settlement, and called it Ephrat. The name is taken from the book of Micah.

"These Jewish settlements springing up on Arab land in the West Bank are the reason for the unrest and subsequent demonstrations. When someone is killed, the

Comforting Arms

Jews dub him a terrorist, but the Arabs call him a martyr. So there you have it, the two sides of the coin.

"There are both Jewish and Arab terrorists. Recently, five Arab buses were suspected and a search revealed a bomb planted in each of them. If they had exploded at the Arab bus station where they were timed to go off, hundreds might have died. Jewish terrorist rings exist in many cities and settlements.

"On Saturdays, their day off from work, the Jews used to come and shop in Bethlehem because the fresh fruit and vegetables were less costly than in their own stores. However, Arab merchants usually keep three prices for their customers: the highest for tourists, next for Jews and cheapest for fellow-Arabs."

"That's not fair," stormed Lisa, "not fair at all. I certainly will not buy anything from the Arabs if that's the way they treat us!"

Abby wanted to refuse to comment, but she felt the rest of her team deserved an explanation for her partiality.

"I sympathize with the Arabs, because God has put in my heart a special love for them. I understand their situation. Many of them have lost their jobs due to the fighting, and they can barely eke out a living for their families. When there is trouble, the Israeli army levels a curfew and closes Arab shops. Tourists cannot visit the area, and this means a loss of profits for the merchants. Families are loyal, and they loan each other money for expenses. To compensate, young Arab men are leaving the country to find work elsewhere. They send most of their wages back to relatives to ensure their survival.

"Jewish settlements built on Arab property are the bone of contention between the two sides. Whose land is it? Arabs have lived on and owned their land for centuries. Now it is being taken away from them. They feel they must fight for what they believe rightfully belongs to them.

"We have time to shop in one of these souvenir stores. Local craftsmen carve many of the items from olive wood because the trees are readily available. Other things, like those Bible covers and jewelry, are mother-of-pearl. The abalone shells are imported from Australia and California but the exquisite filigree work is done here.

"This is a good store and prices are relatively reasonable, considering that if people can afford to tour the Holy Land, they should be able to pay for the privilege. The quality of the merchandise is fine, and the proprietor is a long-time friend of mine. He'll give you a handsome discount."

Colin bought a magnificent olive wood manger scene. "Won't our children be surprised when we set this up at Christmas time? I can hardly wait to see their happy little faces!" Megan bubbled enthusiastically, her copper curls bouncing along with her rotund little body as she anticipated their delight.

Andrew and Cindy settled for elegant jewelry and a Bible with mother-of-pearl covers. Lisa slowly and meticulously looked at everything and decided to forego purchasing anything from an Arab.

Peter and Abby sipped small cups of thick, black Turkish coffee offered by the friendly manager, and waited patiently.

"Tell me more about the situation here. Lisa isn't near so you can be candid," Peter said.

Abby replied, "When we first came, terrorists were quietly at work planting bombs in unusual places: one exploded in a refrigerator on a main street of Jerusalem, another in a loaf of bread on a shelf in a supermarket, others on Israeli buses. Of course, there is always retaliation according to the Bible, 'an eye for an eye, a tooth for a tooth.' Within a few hours following an Israeli bus incident, five bombs detonated among the Arabs, killing several and wounding others. In seven months, more than sixty bombs did their devastating work.

"You can understand why there is good reason for the many army checkpoints we encounter, with thorough searches made of vehicles and of suspected individuals. In one day we were stopped seventeen times and we waited in line from five minutes to half an hour or longer at each place. That was exasperating as well as exhausting. But we understood the purpose.

"Whenever Jewish soldiers saw our American passports they wanted to know why we were driving a car with a blue West Bank license plate. The Jews have yellow plates, Arabs from the Gaza Strip have silver. We explained that we worked in an Arab church, and they usually waved us on."

"I'm sure you've had many experiences of God's protection."

"Yes. One day I was driving along a road skirting Bethlehem and without warning, I hit an oil slick. I didn't know what it was and I braked, the car skidded, fishtailed and landed right on the edge of the mountain behind a car that apparently had done the same thing. Another car slid off the edge, flew into the air, tumbled down the mountain and landed on the roof of a house below."

"Someone must have been praying for you."

"Definitely."

Peter noticed that Abby's hair was beginning to turn gray and guessed her to be close to his own age, perhaps a few years younger. *Yes,* he thought, *her big brown eyes sparkle when she smiles, leaving wrinkles less noticeable except those at the corners of her eyes. She's a small person but decidedly energetic. Her unusually cheerful, patient attitude has to be a gift from the Lord. Nothing seems to perturb her, not even Lisa's sarcastic comments. Already I admire her courage and fortitude. She's a remarkable woman.*

At the same time, Abby was observing Peter. His pleasant grin and twinkling blue eyes made her think he might be ready for mischief and fun at a moment's notice. His dark hair waved slightly and his features gave the impression of strength and stability. His athletic frame looked ready for action and adventure, and he appeared capable of efficiently dealing with whatever the day might bring. He had already been helpful in explaining Biblical truths. In time, God would reveal His purpose in sending this man to join their group.

Chapter 4

The Fields of Boaz

The group rode down a steep, paved road from Bethlehem. Olive groves covered the rolling hills. Sheep and goats grazed on tufts of grass between the gnarled and twisted trees where a shepherd played his flute.

"That must be how David took care of his father's sheep on these very hillsides!" remarked Colin. "I like that flute. I'd like to buy one for my son."

"I saw a boy selling them when I was in Jerusalem," Abby said. "You might find one there."

"David had a slingshot, too. Would they have any like the kind he used?"

"I know where you can buy one," Abby answered. "We can go to that shop later. Right now we're on our way east of Bethlehem to Shepherd's Fields, on the outskirts of this village we're passing through."

Sam stopped the van opposite a field where a shepherd was tending a large flock. Some of the sheep huddled quietly under the shade of a big olive tree. Goats standing on their hind legs reached up into tall bushes to nibble leaves.

Andrew and Colin pulled out their cameras to capture the scene. "What a treat! To see shepherds doing exactly what their forefathers must have been doing when the angels gave them the message of Jesus' birth!" exclaimed Colin.

"These are also called The Fields of Boaz," Abby pointed out.

"So Ruth would have gleaned here. What a romantic place!" Cindy grinned, "I adore that beautiful love story. It's one of my favorites."

"That's my dear wife, Sentimental Cindy," chuckled Andrew.

"It's lunch time. Let's spread these quilts under an olive tree and relax." Abby opened the cooler Julia had prepared. She handed around sandwiches, fruit, cookies and lemonade.

"This is living! No hurry, no driving to work in snarled traffic, no deadlines to meet at the office, no employee peering over my shoulder trying to pry into what I'm putting on my computer. I'm glad to be away from it all. Maybe I should have been born in a Judean village." Colin breathed a deep sigh of relief and stretched out his big, husky frame full length.

After a brief rest, they drove for a few miles on old, narrow asphalt roads bordered by wheat fields. "Look," Cindy exclaimed, "there's a woman riding a donkey and a man walking beside them, like the picture of Mary and Joseph we see on our Christmas cards!"

"Colin, I'd really like a video of that," Megan said quickly.

"Let's ask them, first," Abby suggested. She inquired in Arabic and the man nodded agreement. "Thank you. Here's a little book about God." She handed him a gospel of Luke and he accepted it.

"That scene will have special significance for us," Colin said. "They now have God's word telling them the story of Joseph and Mary."

"May the Lord use it to open the eyes of their understanding," Peter said.

"Exactly," Abby agreed. "You know, the government has passed an anti-conversion law prohibiting anyone from taking any action that would cause someone to change his religion. There is a penalty of five years in prison or a fine of $3,000. It also prohibits a person from receiving anything for the same purpose, with a jail sentence or a fine as punishment. This is aimed at religious groups who offer a free education or money or a spouse to someone if they will convert. It does not apply to us because we do not use bribes."

"Are you saying that there are organizations or cults who do this?" asked Peter.

"I'm afraid so. We know of some who have been sending young people abroad to be trained free of charge. They must then serve their benefactors for X number of years in payment. Unfortunately or otherwise, when the student lives in a foreign country, he encounters temptation. He can marry there, make good money and enjoy a luxurious lifestyle. Why should he leave it to return here?"

"That's easy to understand," Colin sympathized. "I can't really blame them."

They had driven only five miles but it took more than fifteen minutes because the narrow road wound between fields and villages.

"Up ahead is Herodion," Abby said. "It's the remains of one of King Herod's palaces built by slaves on a large man-made hill. Tradition tells us he lavished wealth inside and outside the edifice, and was buried there in a solid gold bier studded with precious stones. His body was dressed in a purple robe with a crown of gold on his head, encircled by a diadem. But all that was long gone hundreds of years ago.

"We can climb that curving dirt path to the top and view miles of Judean countryside crisscrossed with low stone walls. Then we'll go down steps to the inside of the castle."

Sam deposited them halfway up the slope. Abby led the way.

"I need a supporting arm to lean on," Lisa demanded. Again, Peter offered his.

And again Abby noticed the smug smile on Lisa's face. Step two in that relationship? She wondered what the next would be. Not that it mattered to her. Or did it?

The Fields of Boaz

Abby paused at the top, ostensibly to enjoy the view so familiar to her. Her thoughts needed direction and she quietly talked to the Lord from her heart. *You know how I feel without someone to share my life and my love. There is no one else I need to consider, to help and make happy, to 'give and forgive,' my definition of a good marriage. No companionship, no one to depend upon, to make important decisions. No comforting arms around me, no shoulder to lean on. Like Peter, I admit deep loneliness. I believe it can only be healed if I were to marry again. If that is Your plan, Lord, I believe You will send the right man along in Your time and way. I admit I'm attracted to Peter, but so is Lisa. I commit this situation to You. I'm determined to give You priority in all I say and do, always.*

"Where did they get all this stone?" asked Colin as they climbed down wide steps to investigate the ruins of what once had been the throne room, chapel and places for storage, sleeping, bathing and cooking.

"Farmers dig them out of the fields when they clear the land for plowing, and use them to build fences. The larger ones for city structures sometimes are imported from Jordan. Big trucks haul massive chunks of stone to factories where they are cut to size. Smaller pieces are chipped and shaped by hand at the building sites."

Hand in hand, Andrew and Cindy were the first to climb back up the steps to the top. They had the bearing of a king and queen, and a quiet, calm manner that was comforting to the patients they treated. Cindy's light brown hair pulled into a French twist emphasized her elegance. Andrew was over six feet tall and always looked immaculately dressed. He never appeared awkward in spite of his long arms and legs. They were an attractive couple.

Colin and Megan were of a different breed but equally appealing in personality. Their cheery attitude was infectious and their loving relationship admirable. Both men treated their wives with genuine respect and devotion.

Comforting Arms

Lisa clung possessively to Peter as they slowly walked down the circular path to the van. Abby noticed that he appeared to be unaware of Lisa's repeated demands for attention. *Could he possibly be that naïve? Or is he just being polite? Her intentions are by no means subtle; in fact, they are brazenly obvious. But Peter seems to be a gentleman, always ready to help anyone in need. At the same time he manages to wear a kind of sympathetic yet non-committal expression.*

It was late afternoon. Their road led through fields toward a small village. Abby heard shots being fired and guessed what might be happening. As they approached a house on the outskirts, a soldier was crouching beside the road with his gun aimed at the building. He motioned to the van and shouted, "Get back! Get back!"

Lisa began screaming hysterically, "What's happening? We're going to be killed! Let me out!" She tried to open the door but Sam instantly pressed the lock. He quickly backed the van, turned around and sped along the way they had come.

"Let me out of here! Help! Where are we going?" Lisa's yelling was earsplitting. Andrew immediately responded with the calmness befitting his medical profession. He reached over and shook her vigorously.

"Stop, Lisa! Stop right now! We are fine and Sam is taking us away from the danger. Get a hold of yourself. Quiet down." His voice was firm yet soothing. Lisa began crying.

"How could you lead us into such a predicament, Abby?" She was trembling and her voice quivered between sobs as she continued, "You said…we would be safe…and well protected. Now I can't believe anything you tell us."

Abby did not answer. She was learning to be patient and remain quiet in spite of the woman's vituperations. In orientation she had explained that the fighting between the Jews and Arabs had escalated and travel was risky.

The Fields of Boaz

Everyone, including Lisa, had agreed to trust her decisions and God's protection.

Sam detoured in a roundabout direction and there were no more incidents. They all were glad to return to the guest home safely and hurry to their rooms.

Lisa failed to appear for dinner, and Abby was reluctant to go to her. She felt actually relieved that Lisa hadn't come. But she knew it was her duty to inquire about her team member. *Help me to exercise Christ-like love,* she prayed silently as she knocked on the door.

"Enter," Lisa called. She was lounging in bed, covering her face with moisture masque. She said with animosity, "So you've finally come. It's about time. I wrenched my shoulder getting out of the shower. It hurts. I need a doctor."

Abby found Andrew and explained. He and Cindy both went to Lisa's room.

"Let me check to see if it's dislocated, Lisa. No, I think not. You may have bruised it a bit. We'll put your arm in a sling if you like, although it doesn't seem to indicate the need."

"I do like and I do need. So do it," she demanded sharply. "And I'm hungry. I won't be joining you at dinner. Bring mine here," she ordered, looking daggers at Abby.

"I'll bring your dinner, Lisa," Abby said. "I'm sorry you can't join us."

"You heard me. Now go!"

Abby returned with a tray of creamed chicken on rice, peas, and spiced peaches arranged attractively with a small vase of flowers. "Here you are, Lisa."

"Do you call that food for an invalid?" was the woman's sarcastic reaction. She knocked the tray onto the floor, spilling everything it contained. "I need a soft diet. See to it!" she demanded.

Abby quietly cleared up the mess and retreated. She asked Julia to order scrambled eggs, toast, applesauce and tea.

"I'll take it to her," Julia offered, and Abby breathed a sigh of grateful relief.

"This has been an exhilarating and informative day. I'm so glad we came!" Megan said as they relaxed after dinner and reviewed what they had seen.

Abby said, "Peter, would you lead devotions tonight and every night from now on? It would be a big help to me."

"I'll be glad to, Abby." He read the Christmas story and quoted the famous verse, "His name shall be called wonderful, counselor, mighty God, everlasting Father, and Prince of Peace." His prayer of thanksgiving for God's protection and loving care was meaningful.

"What a fitting climax. We've had wonderful experiences today!" Cindy said.

Abby felt comforted that no one else was blaming her for the shocking encounter with the soldier who was shooting across the village road in front of them. She thanked the Heavenly Father for so graciously watching over them.

Chapter 5

Old Beersheba

At breakfast the next morning Abby was outlining the trip when a volley of gunshots erupted close by. Lisa screamed and jumped from the table, brushed off dishes that went crashing to the floor, tripped on her chair, knocked it over and dashed from the room.

"Don't worry, please," Julia said. "It's only the Israeli army practicing maneuvers in a field nearby. There's no danger."

"I think you'll be surprised at what we'll see and do today," Abby continued. "When you're ready, please meet me in the lounge." She hurried away and found Lisa in her room, crying hysterically.

"I'm sorry I ever came on this stupid trip," the distraught woman shouted vehemently. "Why didn't you tell me I could be hurt or killed? I can't believe you've brought me into such a dreadful situation. You should be ashamed to subject your friends to these conditions. Were you thinking of the money you'd make? I know you got your plane fare free. What else did they promise you?"

"Please, Lisa. Listen. You're right, any tour guide who brings at least five people does earn a free fare from certain airlines, but I pay my share of board and room and all the expenses that are involved here, just like everyone else.

"Let me assure you that we're not in danger. Julia has explained those shots you heard. The Israeli army is practicing training maneuvers in a neighboring field. They're careful not to endanger the lives of civilians, and we're

Comforting Arms

careful to observe and obey the signs they post about not entering designated areas. We have the Lord to watch over us and nothing can happen that He does not permit. That's our comfort. We don't need to worry as long as we use our common sense and take proper precautions as we travel."

After a lengthy period of silence punctuated with sniffles, Lisa reluctantly agreed to go along for the day. "But I warn you," she ground out between clenched teeth, "the minute I sense any more trouble like this, I'm packing my bags and taking the first plane home. My nerves cannot endure such horrible shocks. And I will demand the return of the money I paid for this trip, a full refund and perhaps even compensation for mental and emotional suffering."

Her tirade continued until they met the others in the lounge. She hurried to Peter and lifted tear-filled eyes, begging for sympathy. "I need your comfort. Please help me." He assured her that there was nothing to fear and they finally got started.

For nearly ten miles the van wound around curves up and down the Judean mountains. Sam carefully drove slowly, between twenty and thirty miles per hour for Lisa's sake, but again she complained of nausea and made him stop twice. She didn't get out of the van, merely took a drink of water and sighed, shoulders slumped. She swiveled around to look at Peter, her big blue eyes wide, inviting and expecting his attention. He understood and smiled sympathetically.

On both sides of the road were vineyards. "There is the valley of Eschol, on our left. Do you know why it is mentioned in the Bible?"

"Why?" Megan asked.

"Remember the two spies Moses sent to look over the land?"

"Caleb and Joshua," responded Cindy.

"This area is famous for growing huge, delicious grapes, both green and purple. In fact, I've held in my hand one cluster so heavy it weighed five pounds."

Old Beersheba

Sam slowed down to let a Mercedes-Benz pass.

"Did you see the picture painted on the side of that taxi?" asked Abby.

"Yes," answered Cindy, "it showed two men carrying a pole with a big bunch of grapes. That must represent the story about Moses sending out the spies to investigate the land of Canaan."

"You're right. That's the official Government Tourist Agency's insignia."

"I saw that on a key chain in the gift shop," Lisa offered, looking directly at Cindy. She advertised her disapproval of Abby by ignoring her completely.

"Oh, look at that donkey. It's carrying a large woman with a child sitting in front of her and another one behind. I feel sorry for the poor animal." Megan looked more closely and added, "I can't believe it! There are three children hanging on each side! That's nine altogether. How can they do that? How can that donkey bear such a heavy load?"

"There's a metal frame for the children to sit on or for packing supplies," Abby answered, "and the animals are trained to carry big loads. This time the supplies are people. One day, I saw a donkey carrying cloth bags on each side with kids in them, but they were not children. They were baby goats! Their furry black heads and long floppy ears were poking out of the bags."

They passed villages and fields and soon Abby announced, "We're in Hebron. David was king here before he went to Jerusalem. It's famous for glassblowing and pottery. Let's walk over and watch that potter's wheel a few minutes. Doesn't it remind you of what Jeremiah said, '...cannot I do with you as this potter? saith the LORD. Behold, as the clay is in the potter's hand, so are ye in mine hand...'"

"We sing a hymn about that, too," Cindy added. "'Have Thine own way, Lord, have Thine own way. Thou art the potter, I am the clay. Mold me and make me, after Thy will, while I am waiting, yielded and still.'"

Comforting Arms

I'm not ready for that. I prefer my own way, Lisa said to herself as they returned to the van.

Sam turned off the main road and followed a busy palm-lined street to the parking area. Steps led to a large, stone, fortress-like building guarded at the door by Jewish soldiers. When Lisa saw them, she shivered and stared reproachfully at Abby until she looked more closely at one of the handsome soldiers. Immediately, she perked up and offered him a coquettish smile.

Colin was interested in their uniforms and helmets and weapons. "Why is the army here with guns?" he asked.

"They try to keep the Jews and Arabs from fighting. Both of them claim Abraham as their Father. His two sons were Isaac and Ishmael, half brothers. The Jews descended from Isaac and the Arabs from Ishmael. They quarreled then and they're still quarreling. It's over land. Both of them claim possession. That's why there is no peace in this country today."

Abby did not tell them that the Jews had desecrated some Muslim holy items, causing violent riots. In retaliation, the Arabs tore up precious scrolls. The government put the city under curfew and no buses were permitted to run for two weeks.

"Could I take their picture?" asked Colin.

"Perhaps. We should ask them." Abby approached the soldiers and inquired, pointing to Colin and his camera. The men agreed and motioned for Lisa to stand between them. She shrank back, terrified of their guns, but they acted friendly, grinned and insisted. She detected admiration in their glance at her figure and long silky hair. So she cheerfully accepted the challenge and posed gracefully, flattered when they put their arms around her.

As they walked through the building, Abby explained, "This is called the Cave of Machpelah. Here are the tombs of Abraham and Sarah, Isaac and Rebecca, Jacob and Leah. We passed Rachel's tomb in Bethlehem. Do you see that tomb covered with a velvet cloth? It is embroidered with

Old Beersheba

an Arabic inscription that says, 'This is the tomb of the prophet Abraham, may he rest in peace.' The ones honoring Sarah and Jacob say the same thing. Look at the fine stone and mosaic work decorating this Muslim mosque. It was built where there once was a Crusader church over the cave. Some say King Solomon constructed the wall with the help of demons!

"Hebrew tradition claims that Adam and Eve lived in Hebron after God expelled them from the Garden of Eden, and they were buried here. Through that small window you can glimpse a stone that bears an imprint of Adam's foot, according to legend."

When they left, Lisa smiled at the soldiers, expecting compliments. They ignored her and she frowned. Colin noticed her disappointment and whispered with the hint of a chuckle, "The guard has been changed, Lisa." She ignored his comment and hurried to catch up with Peter.

In the crowded market, small individual shops offered clothes, fruit, vegetables, sweets, meat, eggs, grain and bread. Megan and Lisa stopped abruptly, their faces frozen with shock! They had spotted a camel's long neck and head hanging from a hook outside the butcher shop! "That meat is very expensive and it's considered a delicacy," explained Abby. From a fruit stand she bought bananas and handed them around for a tasty snack as they returned to the van.

They drove a short distance to Mamre. "Here is Abraham's Oak. The one we're looking at probably sprung from a root of the original. It's where Abraham pitched his tent and three men came to tell him that Sarah would bear his son. In the Middle Ages, people sliced slivers from the tree to wear as charms for protection during their travels. Mamre is also the place where Abraham asked the Lord to spare Sodom and Gomorrah, but because of their wickedness they were destroyed."

They continued traveling south for thirty miles. On both sides of the road were black and brown tents and small cement or tin houses. Along a path, a girl was leading a camel toward a well for a drink. A young boy rode a donkey carrying water cans fastened to its sides. Sheep and goats grazed in harvested fields.

"Who lives in those tents?" Megan asked. "I'd like to see inside one."

"They're called Bedouins," Abby answered. "The word means 'nomad,' someone who wanders from place to place. They need to find graze land for their flocks and herds. Some of them still roam. Others are settled on land that has belonged to their tribe for hundreds of years. Most of them are Muslims."

"Do you think we could visit one of them? I'd love to see what the tents are like and how the Bedouins live," Megan said.

"Yes. You might enjoy getting acquainted with one of the families. My husband and I used to visit them regularly. They are gracious people who always welcome guests. They have a unique sense of humor and they love to tell stories with a surprise ending. Would you like to hear one?"

"Yes!" Megan and Colin chorused together. Andrew and Cindy nodded agreement.

"Once there was a poor woman whose only means of support was raising chickens. Someone was periodically breaking in and stealing them, one by one. The discouraged woman went to the priest, who promptly assured her he would seek out the culprit. On Friday, the Muslim holy day for worship, the priest finished his sermon to the men assembled and concluded with the statement, 'Someone has been stealing chickens from a poor woman of our tribe and I know who it is.' The guilty man wondered how he had been found out. The priest simply said, 'He has feathers in his hair.' Immediately, the thief was the only man who reached up to feel his hair!"

"Clever, Abby. I like that. Tell us another," Megan begged.

"At one time, Mohammed had a total of fourteen wives. To each of them, in secret, he gave a gold ring and he whispered, 'Don't tell anyone else I gave this to you.' Later, he gave a luncheon and invited all his wives. During the course of the meal, one of the women asked, 'Mohammed, which one of us do you love the most?' He dare not name anyone or he'd have a riot on his hands. After deep thought, he answered, 'The one to whom I gave the gold ring!' Smug smiles ensued, as you can imagine."

Sam turned off the main highway and followed a narrow road leading to a small hill. At the foot of it was a large, deep well. "This was dug by Abraham. Now we'll see the ruins of Old Beersheba, the original town he built." Abby led them up a stony path to the top of the hill.

Again Lisa grabbed Peter's arm for assistance and he willingly obliged.

"Archaeologists have meticulously unearthed the ruins of these mud-brick rooms. Centuries of blowing sand had covered them completely."

"So Abraham lived here several thousand years ago, just as the Bible says," murmured Peter in awed tones. "In Wales I teach Biblical Geography and now I'm seeing where the events took place. Thanks for including this on our tour, Abby."

At the bottom of the hill was a small museum. Cindy bought some pretty little beaded key chains made by the Bedouins. "These will make nice presents for my friends," she decided.

"You're right. That's a good idea," Megan agreed as she picked some out.

Lisa pursed her thin lips scornfully and turned away. "It's hot here. Let's move on, Abby."

"As you wish."

"Tell us another story while we drive, Abby," Cindy suggested.

"Alright. It's only a mile to the new city of Beersheba so there's time enough. A Bedouin caravan was traveling a lengthy route and someone was stealing supplies from the packs the donkeys carried. The men complained to the chief. 'Never fear. I'll find out who it is,' he assured them. That night he announced, 'You all know that my donkey is a descendant of Mohammed's donkey. He's very clever. I'm going to tie him in my tent. Line up, and one by one you must enter the tent and touch the donkeys' tail. When the guilty man touches it, the donkey will bray.' The drivers obeyed and took turns entering the tent. The night was quiet. Everyone listened expectantly. Not a sound came from the donkey. After the men emerged, the chief said, 'Now line up again and put out your hands.' He slowly walked down the row and sniffed each man's hand. 'Here's the thief,' he said, pointing to one of the men. How did he know who the guilty man was?"

"That's a good question, a brain-teaser," Colin said. "Tell us."

"The chief had rubbed fresh mint leaves on the donkey's tail. Every man's hand smelled of mint except the robber's."

"Of course! He was afraid to touch the donkey's tail because he thought it would bray like the chief said. That's a good one, Abby," Andrew said. "Your Bedouins have keen insight."

"Maybe we could use some of their wisdom when we discipline our children, Megan," Colin suggested. "What do you think?"

"It's worth a try," she laughed. "I like the idea."

Chapter 6

New Beersheba

Abby explained that their next stop would be the weekly market near the new city of Beersheba. "A few years ago it was a place where Bedouins traded their sheep, goats, donkeys and camels. At the far end they still carry on the custom, but now here in front, Jewish merchants loudly advertise their wares, shouting for customers to buy souvenirs, food, cold drinks and household supplies."

Beyond the hubbub was an extensive display of Bedouin articles--some new, others used. Colin chose a silver-handled curved dagger. "Will I have a problem taking this on the plane?" he asked Abby.

"I think not, as long as you pack it in a suitcase to be sent with other luggage, and not in your carry-on," she replied.

Megan picked out a pretty black dress embroidered in exquisite cross-stitch with a variety of bright colors and designs. Andrew and Cindy settled for a unique brass coffeepot. Lisa saw nothing to please her finicky taste.

Trucks, buses, vans, taxis and cars clogged the streets of Beersheba. They stopped outside a building with a plate glass window displaying an attractive array of books and souvenirs. Abby introduced them to the manager, and they browsed among the neat shelves. Peter found a version of the Bible he had been wanting and lost no time purchasing it.

"Upstairs is our assembly room for Jewish believers. I'll show it to you if you wish," the manager suggested. They climbed narrow stairs to a large room filled with chairs. A piano, accordion, guitar and drums stood in front. "We meet on Saturdays, our only day off from work."

"Not on Sunday?" Lisa frowned.

"No. There are three holy days observed in this country: Friday for the Muslims, Saturday for the Jews and Sunday for the Christians. On Friday at sundown all the Jewish buses are parked and they'll not run again until sundown on Saturday. You have to remember which day the buses run or you might get stranded!" he laughed.

"We sometimes have four languages being translated from English or Hebrew during our meetings. Jewish believers from many countries have settled here. There are immigrants, friends and visitors from Russia, Finland, Romania, Spain, France, Ireland, Canada, America. Of course we use Hebrew primarily. The young people pick it up easily, but the elderly like to continue using their mother tongue."

"Tell us," Andrew asked, "are there other groups like this in the Holy Land?"

"Oh, yes. There are many, in most of the large towns and in the big cities. There are thousands of Jews who believe that Jesus is the Messiah, and they love and worship Him as their Savior.

"But of course there is persecution so we have to be careful. Our front window has been smashed three times and in the last episode, the building was set on fire. All of our books and supplies were destroyed.

"In Jerusalem a church was burned. Another was broken into but they doused the fire in time and no damage was done. So the terrorists tried again. This time they turned on a hose and the water ruined the carpet and piano. In a Christian cemetery, the crosses on the graves and the headstones are smashed periodically. Believers are threatened, often with phone calls. Some of them lose their jobs because they refuse to take bribes or alter records. Others become disillusioned with conditions and leave the country. Like the Bible says, we have to be 'wise as serpents and harmless as doves.'"

"I had no idea this was happening. We hear about persecution in Europe, Russia, and other countries. But here, too? I'm so sorry. What can we do to help?" asked Cindy.

"Pray for us. We need spiritual stamina to withstand the 'onslaughts of the enemy.'"

"That we can and will do," Peter assured him. "We are all brothers and sisters in Christ."

"We should go now," Abby urged. "Sam is parked in front and he can't stay there any longer or the police will ticket him."

They stopped at a sidewalk café for lunch and while they waited to be served, Megan entertained them with anecdotes about her children. "When their Granny had surgery for a knee replacement, we took Joe and Gina to visit her in the hospital. Joe insisted on taking Colin's metal detector to see if it would work. He dragged it above Granny's new knee and it beeped!"

"That could have been caused by the staples we use for suturing incisions," Andrew commented.

"Undoubtedly," Megan agreed. "But when Gina saw how swollen the knee was, she said, 'Granny, I think they gave you the wrong size knee. This one's too big. They should have given you a smaller one!'"

They all laughed hilariously and even Lisa could not suppress a slight smile. Megan continued, "Would you like to hear a few unique tidbits Joe brought home from school? The children were asked to complete some common proverbs. A few of their answers were, 'Never underestimate the power of…termites. Don't bite the hand that…looks dirty. The pen is mightier than the…pig. Where there's smoke there's…pollution. Children should be seen and not…spanked!'"

"Well done!" Peter laughed heartily. "They certainly made it sound logical."

The waiter came and Abby suggested they order something light because Julia was planning a chicken dinner. "While we wait I can tell you another Arab story if you'd like."

"By all means, please do," begged Megan.

"A hungry priest gave a little boy money and instructed him to go to the village oven and buy a roasted sheep's head for his lunch. The child obeyed but on his way back he caught a whiff of the fragrant aroma issuing from the package. Slowly he peeked into a corner of the newspaper wrappings and glimpsed an ear slightly protruding. It looked so tempting the boy couldn't resist. He took a tiny bite, then another and another, and soon the ear was completely gone.

"'Now this sheep looks lopsided,' he said, and glanced at the other ear. 'I'd best even it up.' So he did. But while he was enjoying the second ear, he noticed the eyes. 'Mmm, what a delicacy,' he thought. 'Surely I can taste one.' And he did. Then, of course, he had to eat the other one to give the sheep balance. Now nothing is quite as good as tongue, the boy decided, and he quickly gobbled it up, too. 'Well, the only thing left is the brain. I might as well enjoy it,' he said. So he did.

"Realizing what he had done, the boy hurriedly rewrapped the sheep's head and ran to the priest. 'Here's your lunch,' he said, more bravely than he felt.

"The priest unwrapped the head, inspected it carefully and complained, 'This sheep has no ears!'

'It was deaf,' the boy answered.
'And what happened to the eyes?'
'It was blind.'
'But where is the tongue?'
'It was dumb.'
'And it has no brains!'
'Oh, sir, it was a priest!'"

"What a story!" Peter chuckled.

"I'm getting hungrier by the minute," Colin said. "Can you hear my stomach rumbling?"

Abby laughed, "No, Colin, we can't. Do you know what the Arabs say about that?"

"Tell us," urged Megan.

"'In my stomach the frogs are croaking!' Some say, 'the birds are chirping.'"

"Well, that's what they're doing," Colin declared. "Ah, here it comes, at last! Hamburgers and French fries!"

"I can tell you some interesting medical definitions while we eat," Andrew offered. "Are you game?"

"Only if they won't make me nauseous," Lisa answered.

"No, they won't. They're just humorous." Cindy smiled and he proceeded.

"Artery means the study of fine painting. Barium is what you do when CPR fails. Caesarean section is a district in Rome. Colic means a sheep dog. A coma is a punctuation mark. To dilate means to live long. Medical staff is a doctor's cane. Organic is a church musician. Varicose veins means veins that are close together. Shall I continue?"

"No, don't," Lisa begged. "Now I do feel sick. I can't eat."

Abby said, "Did you notice the printing on the caps of our Coke bottles? It says, 'kosher.' That means it has been pronounced ritually clean and sanctioned for consumption by a Jewish rabbi.

"Now, if you all are finished, we'll drive past Gerar, where Abraham and Isaac both had similar experiences with the King by claiming that their wives were their sisters. God wonderfully intervened for Sarah because she was destined to bear Isaac.

"Today this area of Gerar has become a Bedouin town. Let's drive through it, Sam. The Israeli government has urged wandering Bedouins to settle into villages like this so their land can be used for agricultural purposes. We were visiting a friend in his newly built house and I asked if he liked this way of life. He sat down cross-legged on the sofa and replied emphatically, 'No.'

Comforting Arms

"I asked him why. He answered, 'When it rains, it sounds like bullets blasting the tin roof.' He preferred a tent. But his wife was very happy with her little bottled gas stove. It saved her the drudgery of gathering wood for cooking; one less chore when she was required not only to care for the family but to put up and take down the tent and pack all their possessions onto camels for the next move to find pasture for their animals.

"The Bedouins are building lovely homes. There is one on stilts, with a cow and chickens underneath, like you suggested when we talked about Jesus' birth, Colin. After they save enough money, the parents add a lower apartment to accommodate the oldest son, who is their social security in old age."

"Where do they get the finances for such large places?" Colin asked. "They certainly cannot keep herds of camels or flocks of sheep and goats in a town this size."

"No, they can't. Many of them have sent their sons overseas to train for a profession. Saudi Arabia, England, Australia and America offer tempting opportunities. When they begin working as engineers, doctors, teachers or bankers, they send money home to their parents. This is how they can afford such luxury.

"We'll go on now to Ashkelon, a principal port beside the Mediterranean Sea. It was occupied by Canaanites during Samson's time. David mentioned it when he lamented over Saul and Jonathan's death. It was the birthplace of Herod the Great. His sister lived there and Herod beautified it with colonnaded courts. There are still some impressive statues dating from the Romans.

"We can stop here in Ashkelon for a swim in the sea before we go on to Ashdod. It's safe and there are life guards."

Lisa donned a suit in shades of blue to match her eyes, and paraded along the beach. Abby watched her closely and tried to analyze the woman's behavior. *She must have been a model at one time, and she still could be if she did not wear that bitter, hardened expression. Perhaps it's a mask hiding disappointment or pain. I must be more patient and tolerate her outbursts sympathetically. 'Pray for one another' applies to her.*

They splashed and swam until Abby suggested they have tea and refreshments. It was cool in the restaurant.

"What? Ice for my tea? Yes. Make it double!" Lisa breathed a sigh of relief. "At last!" she said with irony and a stony look at Abby.

They relaxed and chatted amicably until Abby suggested that Sam drive them through the orange groves. She pointed out historical ruins and said, "Philistines, Israelites, Greeks, Romans, Crusaders and Muslims in turn have occupied this city. The prophets Jeremiah, Amos and Zephaniah mentioned cutting off the inhabitants of Ashkelon. It was one of the principal cities of the Philistines. The Muslims called it 'the Bride of the East.' Merchants profited in trade. Muslims eventually destroyed the town when they fought the Crusaders. Excavations have uncovered these statues and columns, but there are undoubtedly many more to be found.

"Now on a few miles up the coast to Ashdod. The incident we are familiar with is about the Philistines who carried away the Ark of God when they defeated the Israelites, and placed it in their temple next to the god, Dagon. The next morning they found their god fallen over with his face on the ground before the Ark. His head and the palms of both hands were broken off and only the stump of the body was left. The people were shocked! God began destroying them and punishing them with disease until they realized it was His hand upon them. Then they were relieved to send the Ark on to Gath. The story continues..."

Quickly, Lisa interrupted. "Ugh, I hate stories like that! Why not tell us something pleasant? Do we have to be so morbid?"

"Perhaps you'd like hearing about the beautiful mosaics discovered in Beit Guvrin. We don't have time to stop there but we'll drive past. One mosaic shows birds and two deer. Another represents a hunt, symbols of the seasons of the year and a number of animals: a stag, dog, lioness, ram, boar, bear, lion, leopard and antelope. The mosaics are in a Jerusalem museum now.

"We're passing the ruins of a Crusader church," Abby pointed out. "Arabs used to live in them when they were still inhabitable. We're nearing the excavations in Maresha. Peter, would you read about this for us so we'll be prepared when we arrive at the site?"

"Of course. Here we are: 'And Rehoboam dwelt in Jerusalem and built cities for defense in Judah.' I recognize some of these he mentions: Bethlehem, Tekoa, Gath and Mareshah, along with others. Then it says, 'And he fortified the strongholds, and put captains in them, and store of victual, and of oil and wine. And in every several city he put shields and spears, and made them exceeding strong, having Judah and Benjamin on his side.' It sounds like he was preparing for war with the other ten tribes.

"The story goes on to say that King Rehoboam 'desired many wives' and actually had eighteen, along with sixty concubines, and produced twenty-eight sons and sixty daughters. He dispersed his children throughout all the fenced cities of Judah and Benjamin, and gave them plenty of provisions. But, like King Solomon, after he had established and strengthened his kingdom, he abandoned the law of the Lord.

"We can guess what happened. The king of Egypt invaded with horsemen and chariots and captured all those fortified cities. Then he attacked Jerusalem and carried away the treasures of the Temple as well as those in the King's house, even the gold shields Solomon had made. Eventually King Rehoboam turned to the Lord and humbled himself. And as always, when we do that, the merciful Lord forgives."

"Always?" asked Lisa bitterly.

New Beersheba

"Yes. Always. He is our loving Heavenly Father. He forgives and tells us we must also forgive. You know, in the Lord's Prayer we say, 'Forgive us our sins as we forgive those who sin against us.'"

"That I cannot do," she answered emphatically. "Not even if he begs for it."

So she has been hurt badly. Peter's thoughts echoed Abby's. *She needs help during this rough, distressing period of her life. We must use wisdom and faithfully pray for her.*

"Here we are," Abby pointed to the top of a hill overlooking the whole area. "We can climb…"

"Oh, not more climbing! I'm sick of seeing these old ruins from the ancient days. I'll stay in the van. The rest of you can wear yourselves out if you like. Peter, why don't you stay here with me? We can talk," Lisa suggested.

"Sorry, Lisa. I'm interested in all of these Biblical sites. See you later." He wanted to help the woman but he knew he'd better use wisdom and tact. To stay alone with her might lead to an unpleasant situation in which he would need to use extreme caution and strong self-control. He quickly joined the group as they observed the ancient wall with its bastions and the layout of the streets and remains of buildings.

"The area is surrounded by caves and there is a Columbarium, like a funeral parlor, with nearly two thousand niches in its walls for keeping crematory urns. The name is from Latin and means 'dovecote.'

"East of here are more caves. One has forty-four burial places cut out of the rock, and its walls are painted with various inscriptions. One of them reads, 'Gift of Baal,' the main deity of the Phoenicians.

"We'll go on now, past Lachish," Abby said as they returned to the van.

"It was a fortified city when Joshua camped against it with his troops, but the Lord delivered the city into his hand. Later, King Rehoboam included it as one of his armed strongholds.

"There is a lot of history involving King Hezekiah. Sennacherib, King of Assyria, invaded Judah and laid siege to Lachish. His soldiers surrounded the fortified walls and used bows and slings and burning torches, along with battering rams. The conquest was a military victory because it opened the way to Egypt. The king had scenes from the battle engraved in the stone walls of his palace in Nineveh."

"Oh, don't bore us with any more history. We've had enough for one day." Lisa turned around in her front seat to stare at Abby, her disgust obvious.

"Right, Lisa. We'll be home soon and you can relax and enjoy that chicken dinner Julia has waiting for us."

After they finished eating, Lisa cornered Peter and walked with him to the lounge, where he led devotions. It had been a long day, and everyone was glad to retire early.

Chapter 7

In a Bedouin Tent

As the van sped south along a smooth road Lisa asked peevishly, "Now why are we traveling the same route again today? You can't fool me. I know my directions. We've been this way before."

Abby answered, "You're quite right, Lisa. But this is the fastest way and we're turning off later." Changing the subject, she said, "Look at the Arabic writing near the license plate on that truck ahead of us. It says, 'Don't drive fast; death is faster!'

"That's rather appropriate for some drivers. My husband and I saw some terrible examples. An Israeli Army jeep came barreling around the corner of a building, skidded on gravel, careened all over the road and headed full speed right toward us. The driver swerved away just in time or he would have smashed headlong into us.

"Another time a big truck came plummeting down a hill on our left and smacked into an oncoming taxi opposite us. My husband quickly jumped to the rescue and hailed a passing vehicle for help. The taxi driver was bleeding and passengers were lying unconscious. Had we been a split-second earlier, the truck would have hit us broadside and we probably would have been killed."

"Someone must have been praying for God to protect you," Peter said.

"Yes, on many occasions we've experienced His guiding hand and loving care. Look, here's another truck.

Comforting Arms

This one says, 'Don't kiss me.'" Everyone laughed at the thought of bumping into it. Everyone, of course, except Lisa.

"How disgustingly childish," she commented. "And where, may I ask, are we going in this deserted place? We've come at least fifty miles. There's nothing here but empty fields and sand. We're not going to see more ruins, I hope. I've had enough of that."

"This will be something quite different," Abby replied.

Sam looked questioningly at Abby and she nodded for him to turn off the main road. He followed a narrow track beside a clump of trees where a Bedouin was walking. The man wore a long black robe edged in gold and a bright red and white headdress held in place by a doubled black rope.

Sam stopped beside the man and Abby asked in Arabic, "Would you like to ride?"

As the Bedouin turned toward them, Lisa saw a dagger fastened to his belt. She shrank back in her seat with a whispered, "Oh no! I'm glad I'm in the front. There's no room."

Hoping the man had not heard her negative comment, Peter quickly offered, "There's room right here for you. Please join us." He moved closer to Colin and motioned for the man to take his vacated seat.

"Thank you. I'm going to my home beyond those hills," the Bedouin answered in English. He climbed into the back beside Peter, who was charmed by the stranger and smiled a friendly welcome.

Megan was quiet, awed and a bit apprehensive. Her thoughts raced as she glanced sideways at him. She had heard wild stories about the Arab nomads of the desert. She wondered what this one was like. What would he do? Could he be trusted? She was curious to see what the Bedouins were like, but now that one was right here, she was not sure how she felt. Why the dagger in his belt? What would he use it for? How dangerous might he prove to be?

Cindy calmly decided that if Abby was willing to risk picking up this stranger, she had no right to question such a decision. *At any rate, there are four strong men in the van who would react immediately to protect the women. Not to worry. Wait patiently and see what will happen. This may very well turn out to be an experience to treasure.*

Lisa's lips were clamped together in a tight line, a frown wrinkling her forehead. She was ready to jump out and run at the least sign of trouble. She turned to stare at the stranger and was on the point of offering her usual negative comments when Peter recognized her intention and quickly spoke up.

"I'm Peter. What is your name?"

"My name is Musa. It means 'Moses' in English," the young Bedouin answered. He asked Sam to bear left along a road of deep sand. The van slowed down to a crawl. Sam shifted into low gear. The wheels churned, whirling dust into thick piles on the windows. Sam could not see anything ahead and turned on the windshield wipers. Dust invaded the van and they all coughed and tried not to breathe it in. Their hair and eyelashes were soon covered with it.

Megan giggled, "Colin, you have gray hair!"

"So do you!" teased Cindy, "and Andrew does too."

"We all have. We look like clowns!" Megan was laughing so hard she nearly fell off the seat. Her merriment was infectious and everyone joined in except Lisa. She was holding a tissue in front of her nose and mouth and meticulously brushing herself off.

The deep sand eventually gave way to solid ground. They bumped and jolted over ruts and around stones and bushes. At last the young man pointed to a group of tents and asked Sam to stop in front of a large one.

"Please come in and have coffee," Moses urged. It was the Bedouin way of expressing gratitude by saying, 'thank you for the ride,' their customary offer of payment for such a debt.

Comforting Arms

An elderly bearded man appeared and welcomed the guests with a smile. Moses introduced him, "This is my father, and he said, 'my home is your home.'" He took off his shoes before entering the tent, so the group followed his example and removed theirs. Lisa balked at the indignity but finally succumbed to custom and slipped off her sandals.

The old man motioned for them to sit on foam rubber mattresses covered with bright flowered cloth. A woman emerged from the back of the tent and warmly greeted the ladies with a kiss on both cheeks. She brought big fat pillows like bolsters for them to lean on.

Cindy was fascinated with the woman's black, colorfully embroidered dress, like the one Megan bought in the Beersheba market. Her white veil had tiny flowers threaded through it. Tattoo marks decorated her forehead and chin. Her ears were heavy with silver rings and her left nostril was pierced with a large, thin gold hoop bearing a wide dangling ornament. How would she ever eat, with that huge nose-ring hanging down in front of her mouth? She's probably used to dealing with the obstacle and it's no problem, Cindy decided.

The woman wore a variety of colored beads, a heavy amber necklace and wide silver bracelets. Her hair was held back with silver clips and hung in two thick braids.

"Please meet my mother. And my brothers and sisters," Moses added as several children appeared and shyly stole glances at the guests.

"Tell us their names," Megan suggested.

"I'm the oldest. There is Samia, then Karim, Rafiq, Sammar and Shakar. Not all of them are here. My mother had eleven children. When she had no more, my father took a second wife. She has twelve. Now he teases both wives by saying he is hunting for a third. This is how he keeps them obedient."

"That's a big family to support," said Andrew.

"A Muslim must be able to take care of his family. Each wife lives in a separate tent. The others in this camp belong to my uncles and their families. As the sons mature, we help with chores, shepherding and expenses. A famous sheikh from our tribe, during his lifetime, had a total of forty-one wives and three hundred children."

"I didn't know so many wives were permitted by the Koran," Colin said.

"The rule is only four at a time. But if the woman does something to displease her husband, he only has to repeat 'I divorce you' three times, and she must leave and return to her father or a male relative who will look after her until he can marry her off again."

Disgusting. No woman should have to endure that kind of life. I certainly would not! Lisa decided. *No one is ever going to tell me what to do or where to go.*

Megan was sitting near the cloth of the tent and felt it with her fingers. A goat poked its head in and out through a hole to nibble grain from a bowl beside her. She giggled and Cindy smiled at the sight. Then she asked, "How is this cloth made?"

"My mother and aunts spin the wool of our sheep and goats and camels into yarn. They weave it into lengths on a loom and then they sew the pieces together. Come with me. My aunts are weaving now. They'll show you how it's done."

The ladies immediately responded and followed Moses to the next tent. Outside it were several women taking turns with the shuttle. It took nearly five minutes to weave one strand of yarn across the three-foot width and snug it up tight. Little children and chickens walked all over the long length of thick finished cloth, leaving dusty footprints. No one seemed to mind. One of the women handed the shuttle to Abby.

"Try it," Moses urged. She knelt down, but her fingers tangled up the threads. With a grin, she handed the shuttle to Cindy. She also had trouble. Megan tried but she was awkward, too. Lisa refused. They thanked the ladies and chattered happily as they returned to the tent.

Comforting Arms

Abby said, "There is an Arab expression, 'You can't put a tent over your head.' It means, 'You can't hide from God!'"

Moses nodded and turned to Abby. She said, "My husband and I used to visit friends here to tell them about God's love."

Moses hesitated. "Ah, yes, now I remember. You gave my father a book called, 'The Holy Scriptures.'"

"That's right. The Word of God. Did you read it?"

"I did. I waited a long time for that book. I'm still reading it."

"What do you think of it?" Peter asked.

"It is good. It tells about God like the Koran does."

"And God's great love for us. That is the key to understanding Christianity."

"Yes, and I have the little book you gave us, too. The colors of the pages tell a story: black for sin, red for Jesus' blood shed when He died on the cross, white for a clean heart and gold for heaven."

Abby nodded. "The Wordless Book. I'm glad you remember. It is a personal message, you know. Do you believe it in your heart?"

"Yes. I do. I have believed it ever since I studied the part of the Holy Scriptures called the New Testament. It tells about the sinless life of Jesus and that God loves us so much He sent Jesus who died to save us from our sin. Then He rose again and today He lives in heaven to hear and answer our prayers. I found this concept in no other religion I have investigated. It gives me forgiveness and peace in my heart."

"I'm so glad, Moses. I hope you will share this with your family."

"I have done that. My father and mother are convinced that Jesus is 'the Way, the Truth and the Life!'"

Abby and Peter both nodded and smiled with pleasure. Here was a Bedouin family they would meet in heaven someday. What unmitigated joy!

In a Bedouin Tent

"Where did you learn to speak English?" asked Andrew.

"In school. But we have no one to speak it with so my accent is faulty."

"You speak very well," Andrew said, and meant it.

A young woman carrying a tiny baby joined them. Abby immediately held out her arms. The infant was wrapped in 'swaddling clothes' like a little papoose and squirmed a bit, then relaxed. Abby felt the result as warm liquid seeped through her long skirt! She said nothing, grinned and looked contented. Peter noticed the beautiful expression on her face and caught his breath. *This woman is one in a million. I want to know everything about her. Is she the reason I've come on this trip? God, give me wisdom.*

"Did you know," Moses said, "that a child sometimes exists on what the camel provides? It may be born behind a resting camel, weaned on its milk, eat the butter, be dressed in warm camel-skin clothes, sleep in a tent made of its wool and ride on it. The camel is a Bedouin's most prized possession."

From where she sat, Megan could observe the animals outside. "There are camels, sheep, goats, donkeys, chickens and a duck, as well as several lambs and dogs. But the dogs look odd. Oh, I see! It's their ears. What happened to them?"

"We always cut off their ears when they are born. It makes them better watchdogs," explained Moses.

"They look more vicious, too," Cindy decided, "but I guess that's no worse than cutting off their tails like we do in America."

While Moses' mother prepared coffee in a blackened brass pot over a small crackling fire in the ground in front of them, a little newborn lamb climbed into Megan's lap. She sat very still and gently petted its soft curly wool and long floppy ears until it contentedly fell asleep.

Lisa was silent. Her face showed disapproval of the situation but she refrained from voicing her opinion. Abby was relieved that she would not have to apologize for the young woman's embarrassing behavior.

Moses talked with Peter about peace. He picked up a bit of earth between his thumb and finger. "My father says when we die we can't take this much land with us."

"True. Some day Jesus, the Prince of Peace, will come. He will bring lasting peace to the Earth. Until then, we can have the peace He gives in our heart, like you have found."

Moses agreed and translated for his father. The old man nodded his head and proceeded to serve the thick, strong coffee in china demitasse cups. Lisa refused to drink it. Quickly Abby explained that the lady was unable to tolerate coffee, so their host would not be offended by her refusal. The others were surprised but pleased when their cups were filled three times, according to Bedouin custom.

"I notice your neighbor has a TV antenna sticking up out of his tent," Colin said.

"Yes, it's run by a generator. At night we all gather to watch the news and the programs from Egypt and Jordan."

When the guests stood to leave, Moses' mother brought a dozen eggs and gave them to Abby. It was her way of thanking the guests for their visit. Abby responded with the customary parting wish, "May God increase your wealth."

The entire Arab family walked to the van with the visitors and kindly invited them come again. Abby thanked them for their gracious hospitality and said they would be happy to return.

"I loved that visit. I hated to leave," Cindy said as they drove away.

Lisa exploded with disgust. "The tent was dirty, animals and chickens prowled and pecked around inside, the children looked ragged and their hair was uncombed. We sat on the ground on mattresses with who knows how many bugs crawling onto our clothes. Those cups you drank out of were far from clean. And you liked it? How in the world could you? It was a despicable experience I hope never to repeat."

Cindy interrupted the tirade, "You have a right to your opinion, Lisa. But the rest of us will treasure this introduction to a culture so vastly different from our own. It's a unique visit we'll always remember."

Megan added, "The children were adorable. I wonder if they go to school?"

"Yes. Many of them do," Abby answered, "especially the boys, when there isn't work for them with the animals or in the fields. They learn to read and write their own language of Arabic. Can you guess what kind of school bus they ride?"

"I haven't seen any like the ones we have at home. I can't think what it might be," Megan frowned.

"Can you guess, Colin?"

"No, I guess not."

"Anyone?"

"Tell us, please."

"A donkey. They ride a donkey to school."

"What fun!" Megan laughed. "Our Joe and Gina would love that, wouldn't they, Colin?"

"Now you've met some of my favorite people. I love the Bedouins dearly. I'm glad God gave me the privilege of visiting them and learning to know their customs. I've wept with them in their sorrows and laughed with them in their joys. They are loyal friends."

"They're living like Abraham lived long ago. And we've met some special, warmhearted friends," Peter remarked. "I think the Scripture promise, 'The desert tribes will bow before him...' is prophetic. Some day the Bedouin tribes of the desert will bow before the Lord. Thank you, Abby, for that visit."

After they returned for a late lunch in the guest home, Abby checked with her friends to see what they would like to do. The two couples opted to shop in Bethlehem again so Sam drove them in. Lisa sarcastically explained that she would have to shower and wash all the clothes she had worn that day to make sure that there were no remnants of the dust and the visit to the Bedouins.

Julia asked Abby to accompany her as she took canned fruit and staples to a needy family in a nearby refugee camp. Peter joined them. They had to pass through a narrow opening between barbed wire and tell the guards whom they wanted to see.

Peter was shocked at the living conditions they encountered. Parents, five or six children, plus aunts, uncles and cousins all lived in one or two rooms patched with cardboard, tin, mud, bricks, stones--whatever was available. They carried water from a community faucet. Because of many curfews imposed due to the fighting, the men were unable to travel to work. As a result, they could not provide for their dependents. Yet in spite of the distressing situation, the family maintained a cheerful attitude and welcomed their guests graciously.

After a brief visit and coffee, the three friends returned to the guest home. Lisa stood in the arched entrance, frowning. "Where have you been, Peter? I need to talk with you. Come."

They headed for a bench beneath the rose arbor, and Julia looked at Abby, eyebrows raised.

"What can I say?" Abby responded. "I know God has a purpose in permitting that relationship,"

"Yes, that He may. But I don't like it."

Chapter 8

The Wilderness of Paran

Abby advised her friends to pack small bags with enough clothes for several days. "We're going to have a long drive," she said, "and bring along your swimsuits."

"Hmm, sounds interesting," Peter said as they ate a hearty breakfast of cereal, toast, hard-boiled eggs, fruit, coffee and tea.

"We've had eggs every day," Lisa complained. "Too much cholesterol, by far."

"It's the custom among Arabs and Jews. They're hard-working people and they burn up a lot of energy. Many of the Jewish kibbutzim are chicken farms so their products are easily available, and they're less expensive, too. Would you like something else? I'll ask Julia to fix it for you."

Lisa thought for a moment. Then she said emphatically, "Well, we're certainly paying enough to be provided with proper nourishing food. But who needs these extravagant meals?" She left the table quickly and was first in the van as it headed south.

"We're going the same direction we went yesterday," the habitual complainer observed sarcastically. "What a waste of gas, and we're the ones paying for it, may I remind you!"

"Yes," Abby admitted, "you're quite right. This is the same road, but it's the most direct route and we're going much farther south."

Beyond the olive groves, shepherds were guiding their flocks along the road. "Look at this," Andrew chuckled, "a living, extremely slow-moving roadblock. I like it!"

"What a bother! Why don't you blow the horn, Sam? They've no right to hold us up like this." Lisa reached over but before she could touch the horn, Sam grabbed her hand. She quickly jerked it away, pursing her lips and frowning at his audacity, unconscious of her own. He looked at her sternly but said nothing, although his meaning was quite clear: *I'm driving this van. Keep quiet. This is my job and I'll do it my way.* He waited patiently until the animals were herded off to one side.

A donkey coming toward them carried a gigantic load of hay. Only its legs and nose showed. "It looks like a wandering haystack!" Megan laughed merrily at the spectacle and everyone joined her.

"You've described that donkey perfectly!" Colin commented.

A woman walking along the roadside balanced a big bundle on her head. It looked heavy and Megan asked, "How can she do that? Why doesn't it fall off? She's not even holding on to it."

"She has a ring shaped like a big doughnut made out of twisted straw and covered with cloth. She puts it on her head and places her load on so it won't slide off. Little girls begin with a small item. Carrying things this way gives them good posture. See how gracefully she walks?"

Hanging down the lady's back was a cloth bag fastened to a long cord wound around her head. Sam drove slowly so everyone could observe her more closely.

"Look, she's sitting down beside the road and slipping the bag from her back. Oh, she's taking out a baby!" cried Cindy.

"I've seen a village woman wrap her baby in a cloth, place it in a big pan and balance it on her head. This leaves her hands free. Over there is a woman spinning yarn as she

The Wilderness of Paran

walks along. She pulls wool from a bag at her side and twists it into yarn as it winds onto the wooden spindle."

They passed scraggly mustard bushes. In the distance, camels and a tent on a hill were silhouetted against the sky. From a well a woman pulled up a bucket tied to a rope and poured water into a trough for her sheep and goats. "You can see that well is very old because over the years the ropes used for pulling up water have worn deep grooves into the rim of stones around the edge."

A large herd of camels blocked the highway. "Here we go again. Another roadblock," moaned Lisa. "I don't understand why these men can't keep their animals off the road."

We should call her, 'The Moaning Lisa.' Megan giggled as the thought flashed through her mind.

Again, Sam quietly and patiently waited for the driver to urge the animals to one side. They were slow, smelly and bellowing loudly.

Lisa pulled out a tissue and covered her nose. "Ugh, I'm glad they are behind us," she muttered as she turned to look back at them. "They should be herded in places where there is no traffic. It's a wonder they aren't hit, the way they wander aimlessly, endangering our safety as well as their own."

Ignoring her remarks, Abby said, "One day the sky was gray and it looked like it would rain any minute. I heard a lot of thunder rumbling. It came closer and closer but there was no rain. I couldn't understand why. The puzzle was finally solved when I looked across the field from my kitchen window. Down the road ambled a large herd of camels! Their noisy grumbling and bellowing sounded exactly like thunder! They certainly had me fooled."

Megan asked, "Abby, could we have a camel ride while we're here? I think it would be lots of fun!"

"What about the rest of you?" Abby asked.

"Yes, by all means," Colin answered. Cindy and Andrew agreed.

"Lisa, are you game?"

"No. Definitely, absolutely not. Only under extreme circumstances could you get me up on one of those horrible, stinking beasts."

"Peter? How about you?"

"I'd enjoy that experience, I'm sure."

"We'll try to arrange it, then."

The farther south they went the hotter it felt. They stopped for a break at a little stall and had sweet tea with mint.

"I want some ice in my tea," Lisa demanded.

"Sorry. There's no electricity here, and no ice for cold drinks."

"How disgusting. I might have known."

"Speaking of electricity reminds me of the time my husband and I were traveling along a road. We saw huge sparks like a fireworks display in front of us. We stopped immediately and found a utility pole lying right across the road, with wires trailing from it. If we had come a few seconds earlier it might have fallen on us. We drove under the wires hanging from the opposite pole, and got through."

"That's another example of God's loving care and protection, eh?" Peter glanced at Abby and she nodded.

Several men sat cross-legged on the sand near the tea stall. One of them fingered what looked like a rosary. "What is he doing with those beads?" Colin asked.

"Those are called 'worry beads.' He's a Muslim, repeating the ninety-nine names of God. The story is told that God actually has one hundred names but only the camel knows the hundredth. He won't tell anyone what it is, and that's why he wears a smirk on his face!

"According to tradition, whoever knows the ninety-nine names will enter into paradise. Many of those names are the same ones that we attribute to God: He is the Creator, Merciful, Compassionate, Holy, Powerful. He hears and answers prayer. He is the Giver of resurrection life, our Friend, Protector, Helper, the One worthy of praise, Eternal,

The Wilderness of Paran

the Judge. Yet of all ninety-nine names, not one of them is...can you think of one they may not know?"

"Tell us," Cindy urged.

"What is one of the first Bible verses you teach children in Sunday School?"

"Hmmm. 'Be ye kind'?"

"That's one the Muslims also know."

"'Love one another,'" Megan offered.

"Yes. Almost. You're close."

"Love. 'God is love,'" Peter said.

"You're right, Peter. Love."

"The basis of our faith!" he exclaimed. "The love of God. We sing about it, write about it, revel in its truth, apply it to our daily living."

"Yes. Sadly, they do not know Him as the God of love. But His love is the heart of Christianity. Some Muslims think of God only as the Judge, the One who punishes for wrongdoing, the One who will decide their fate based upon their good works. They believe that when they die, an angel will perch on each shoulder. One is good, and one is bad. They must walk across a hairline bridge toward heaven. If their bad deeds outweigh the good, the bad angel pushes them off into hell below. If their good works outweigh the bad, the good angel takes them by the hand and pulls them across the bridge into Paradise. There they will enjoy all kinds of physical, sensual pleasures for eternity. But they do not know where they will go until they die.

"One of their famous writers said, 'At the time of death, which road will I take?' A beautiful young Muslim neighbor asked me, 'What will happen to me when I die? I'm afraid.' I was glad to share the answer with her."

"I'm glad I know what will happen to me when I die. I have accepted God's plan of forgiveness for my bad deeds, and I have a clean heart. So I am assured of heaven." Megan's simple statement elicited smiles of agreement from her friends. Lisa was quiet.

"You've put it accurately and succinctly," Peter said.

Comforting Arms

They drove through desolate, sun-scorched desert dotted with scrawny bushes and an occasional thorn tree. A sign read, "Do not leave the road. Hidden mines." Abby explained, "During the fighting here in the Sinai Peninsula, mines were planted."

They passed the rusty remains of an Egyptian tank left in a field near the road.

Another sign warned of army maneuvers. "Firing zone." Farther along, "Firing on the right." Still farther, "Firing on the left." And eventually, "Firing on both sides."

"Stop!" Lisa screamed, and grabbed at Sam. He pushed her away firmly. "No, go on. Fast! Get us away from here. Quickly! I don't believe we are driving through the middle of this terrifying place. How could you expose us to this horrible danger? What are you thinking of, Abby? I demand an explanation."

Colin interrupted her tirade. "Oh, Lisa, don't be so hard on Abby. Calm down. We're safe, aren't we? We haven't seen any soldiers. We haven't even heard guns firing."

"That's no comfort. We could have been hurt or killed. I don't like this. I don't like it at all!" She tossed her blonde hair in angry defiance.

"Don't worry, Lisa. We'll return by a different route. We won't come this way again." Abby glanced at Lisa. Her blue eyes registered fear, then loathing as she glared back.

"Oh, look over there," exclaimed Cindy, changing the subject. She pointed to distant cream-colored mountains topped with brown stones cascading in streams.

"They remind me of scoops of vanilla ice cream with hot fudge sauce dripping down the sides!" exclaimed Megan, licking her lips. "Mmmm, I'd like a sundae like that right now."

Colin smiled indulgently at his wife. "You'll have to wait till we get back home, my love."

"Beyond this vast expanse of deserted flatland are more of those tall, rocky mountains. We'll see them close-up eventually. There are ruggedly beautiful buttes and jagged peaks with layers of multicolored rock, like giant cakes sliced through to reveal deeper colors that change their hues with the sunlight.

"We're crossing one of the places where Moses led the children of Israel when they wandered around in this Sinai Peninsula. They camped here when the spies entered Canaan to reconnoiter. Ishmael, Abraham's son by Hagar, lived here. It's called the Wilderness of Paran. Let's sit under that big palm tree to eat lunch."

While they ate, Peter asked," Would you tell us more about your experiences when you lived here, Abby?"

"Well, one day in this vicinity we drove into a tremendous sandstorm. Sand obliterated the road so we turned and headed west, then south. Still we were in the middle of the storm. On the way we met a couple of boys and gave them a Bible and New Testament. They were cutting across the road to get home. We passed a young girl, and we backed up to offer her a ride. Her lips were caked with sand but she refused our help and kept plodding along. We gave her a gospel and a tract that she tucked inside her long veil.

"We couldn't see ten feet ahead and sometimes not at all. Sand hit the car with a sharp stinging sound, blew inside and covered our clothes, faces and mouths. If we tried to speak, it got into our teeth. Gritty sand came out of our eyes for hours afterwards. The storm lasted three hours. We finally emerged at a checkpoint where soldiers always note a car's license plate.

"'What is wrong here?' one of them asked sternly.

"John immediately jumped out of the car to see what the soldier meant. He explained that we had just been through an extensive sandstorm. When he returned I asked what the problem was. He said all the paint had been blasted off the front license plate! Naturally the soldier wanted to know who we were and where we were from.

"On another occasion we hit a patch of road completely covered by blowing, drifting sand. I was driving and before I could maintain momentum and shift gears, we were stuck. We hopped out and began scraping and digging deep sand away from the tires. My husband drove about a car length and we got stuck again, so again we dug and scraped. We prayed and dug, what I called a combination of 'faith and works.' After repeating this process three or four times, we emerged from that thirty-foot-long stretch of twelve-inch-deep sand and went on our way."

"What an experience!" Colin said. "Tell us more."

"You know the road signs we see along the way? So much sand had blown around one that it was buried nearly five feet deep. We could only see the tip of the top sticking out. We had no idea what it was for."

Troublesome flies buzzed around. Lisa swatted at them nervously. "This is a far cry from a proper restaurant. Aren't there any decent eating places along the way?"

"Not in this area. But we'll have a good dinner in a hotel tonight. I've made reservations for us. Here's a towelette for your hands." Abby passed out packets to everyone. "There are no restrooms here, either. If you need one, over there are sand dunes for privacy." She pointed to several not far away.

Lisa's face registered disgust. Before she could make another cutting remark, Cindy said, "Lisa, remember Abby told us we might be roughing it a few times. This is one of them. It's worth it to be where we are and taste a bit of life as our missionaries live it. I, for one, sincerely appreciate this experience."

"Well, I do not! I don't believe this, Abby. How could you subject us to such indignities? And there is nothing to see but stony mountains and desert sand. It's not only extremely hot but extremely vexing...boring...disgusting. Oh, what's the use? You are responsible for our comfort and safety and you don't perform these duties satisfactorily at all."

The Wilderness of Paran

This time, Andrew jumped to Abby's defense. "That's enough, Lisa. We don't want to hear any more of your complaints. The rest of us are taking the lack of amenities in our stride and enjoying the experience. You've no right to vent your personal frustrations on Abby. If you don't like these trips, stay in the guest home and watch TV or read a book. But please, it's time you stopped this incessant criticizing."

Abby was quiet. She was sensitive to Lisa's sharp comments and felt it best not to answer. Never before had anyone treated her so contemptuously. It was like constantly being bombarded with arrows that pierced her heart. This new experience was a challenge to her courage and faith. Close to tears, she prayed silently, *Lord, help me to endure this cheerfully and graciously. It is a test of my patience and an opportunity to exhibit a humble, graceful, loving Christ-like attitude. I know this is what I must do but it's not easy in the face of her constant comments. I keep thinking of how You would react, what You would say or do. You're my example. May Your Holy Spirit permeate my being so that Lisa can see You are in complete control of my actions and reactions. Help me to forgive her according to Your command to be kind one to another, tenderhearted, forgiving one another, even as God for Christ's sake has forgiven me.*

Peter was keenly aware of Abby's silence and sensed that she might be praying. He prayed that she might continue to exhibit wisdom and a sweet, loving spirit in handling this unusually difficult woman. He also prayed for Lisa, that God would open her eyes to the meaning of a complete surrender of her life to Jesus Christ. Only then could her selfish attitude be changed into an unselfish one and she would become a "new creature," filled with His Holy Spirit.

Chapter 9

The Red Sea

Farther south, the tour group passed a wildlife reserve. Ibex and gazelles stood flicking their tails under the sparse shade of thorny acacia trees.

"A variety of desert animals live in the Sinai Peninsula," Abby explained. "Somali donkeys are a protected species found here and in the deserts of Ethiopia. There are rare antelopes, lynx, addax, oryx, mice, hedgehogs, hares, foxes and bats. Bedouins use camels, goats, sheep and domestic donkeys, as you've already seen. There are lovely birds, too: warblers, the rose finch, plover, raven, horned lark, trumpeter bullfinch, quail, tawny owl and ostrich."

A sign pointed to Solomon's Pillars and Sam turned onto tracks that led along a lengthy sandy valley bordered by colorful mountains. They stopped in front of reddish cliffs formed like huge pillars.

"These are called Solomon's Pillars. Nearby are the remains of an ancient temple, and beyond are old copper mines that were worked by prisoners and slaves. Now modern ones have replaced them but you can still see the old smelting pits and heaps of black slag. You're free to roam about as you like."

In a matter of minutes, Lisa complained, "Let's get out of here, Abby. It's too hot to sightsee. I need an air-conditioned hotel room to rest in right now," and she hurried back to the van. "Well, at least I will stay cool if Sam left the air-conditioner going. Ah, what a relief! He did. I grant you that much foresight. You've little else," she mumbled.

The Red Sea

Abby called to the rest, "Are you all ready to go on?"

"I hate to leave. I'd like to see the smelting pits," Colin said, "but I won't delay you. Some day, though, I want to return and investigate this fascinating enterprise thoroughly."

"It's about time you turned up," Lisa snorted as they got under way. "We had to wait too long. How can you stand this terrible heat? It's like a blast furnace. Very appropriate for the location of those old mines."

Ships were anchored in the harbor of the city they approached. "Where do you think we are?" Abby asked.

"Give us a hint, please," Colin suggested.

"This is the sea where God performed a miracle for Moses as he led the Israelites out of Egypt."

"The Red Sea. Of course," answered Peter.

"It's a beautiful peacock blue, isn't it?" Cindy observed.

"We're driving through the city of Elat. It was an important commercial and military harbor in Biblical times. Crusaders stationed merchant fleets and their navy here. Now it's a bustling city and year-round resort because of its mild, sunny winters and dry summers. It has developed into a busy port. On our left those anchored ships are from various countries. They ply the sea routes to Africa, Asia, the Persian Gulf, the Far East and Australia. Twenty million tons of crude oil are piped from here to a city on the Mediterranean Sea. Those new cars parked near the docks are imported from Japan.

"Here's the underwater observatory. We can walk along that jetty and enter the little building in order to see tropical fish and coral in their own habitat."

They climbed down steps to a big enclosed round room underneath the water and peered through the windows.

"There's a huge shell, and a fish with a long pointy nose!" Megan giggled.

"The shell is a giant clam and the one with the pointy nose is a needlefish," Andrew said. "I'm in my element right

67

Comforting Arms

here! Look over there at the arch made of coral. And see that school of tiny fish swimming past."

"God has given them beautiful rainbow colors, hasn't He?" observed Peter.

"What are those odd black things like small balls with shining beady little eyes and lots of sharp pointed spines?" asked Megan.

"Sea urchins. They sting if you touch them. Be careful when you swim and stay away from them!" Abby warned.

"Here we go again. More danger to beware of," grumbled Lisa.

After an early dinner Lisa announced, "I'm going to relax in my comfortable, cool room and watch television."

The rest of the group eagerly explored the coast. They waded in the water and found a beach covered with small red stones.

"Maybe this is why it's called the Red Sea," Peter guessed, "though some people claim it's because at sunrise the water looks red."

"You're quite right," Abby agreed. "Perhaps both explanations are valid. We can check it out in the morning."

Shops along the streets displayed a variety of shells and objects designed exclusively for the tourist trade.

"Here's jewelry made from the smooth blue-green Elat stone. It's brought from the vicinity of those copper mines we saw, Colin," Abby said.

"Then you must have a ring to remind you about coming back," Megan decided as she chose one. "Here, see if this fits." Colin put it on and gladly paid for it.

One delicate piece of white coral shaped like a castle tempted Cindy. "I love that. It's exquisite."

"Then you shall have it. You deserve it," Andrew said, and promptly bought it for her.

Abby appreciated the loving and caring spirit displayed by these young couples. Andrew and Cindy were a team not only in the operating room but also as husband and

The Red Sea

wife. Colin and Megan seemed like ideal friends and devoted parents. She admired their fine Christian example of what a model marriage should be. No doubt they had their disagreements, knotty problems, even heartaches, but apparently they had learned how to cope with each one amicably.

They returned to the hotel and settled in a secluded corner of the lounge. Abby went to find Lisa and was surprised that she was already in pajamas, her face a ghostly white with cleansing cream.

"You're not coming for devotions?" Abby asked.

"No. I'm tired. I need sleep. Now leave me alone."

"Good night, then. Pleasant dreams," Abby replied.

Peter spoke briefly. "The Red Sea reminds us that God has promised to be with us regardless of how difficult our circumstances may be. He will bring us through victoriously. 'When you pass through the waters, I will be with you...' is one of God's promises."

"I like that analogy," Cindy said. "In our hospital we meet a lot of people who are suffering. This is a good way to comfort and encourage them."

"What a valuable lesson for us to remember," Andrew commented. "Thanks, Peter. I appreciate your insight and the way you apply God's Word to our life today."

Peter thought of Lisa's trying taunts. Abby certainly was passing through difficult waters. His prayer was filled with power and faith in the promises of God's Word.

"Good night, everyone. Sweet dreams," Abby said.

The two couples retired to their rooms. Abby quietly slipped outside and found a comfortable seat where she could watch the moonlight bathing the ripples of the sea. Peter followed and asked, "May I join you?"

"Yes, of course," she answered, and he sat down beside her.

"Abby, tell me more about your experiences when you lived here. There must have been difficult times."

"Yes, Peter. There were. I remembered the verse in

the Bible that says, 'Thou therefore endure hardness as a good soldier of Jesus Christ.' The bumpy old Arab buses I rode in had hard seats!" she laughed. "But that didn't matter. It was the bitter enmity and devastating fighting between the Jews and the Arabs that hurt my heart.

"I was waiting for a bus one day and a grumpy-looking Arab suddenly spit at the feet of a Jewish soldier beside me. A few days later a similar incident occurred but this time the spit was aimed accurately at me. The person who did it probably thought I was Jewish. My mental reaction was, 'Father, forgive him for he knows not what he is doing.'

"In Bethlehem a young boy blew his nose into his fingers, flipped it toward me, and it landed on the sleeve of my coat. He, too, did not realize what he was doing."

"How could you endure such insults?"

"When you know you are where God wants you to be, doing what He has planned for you, that kind of vulgar conduct rolls off your back like the proverbial water off a duck's.

"We gave a gospel booklet to a young boy and when he saw that it was about Jesus, he spit on it and threw it into the gutter. As we left, I looked back and saw him pick it up. It had a beautifully colored cover and was quite attractive, so he must have wanted to take another look!

"It seemed that opposition in one place was balanced by an encouraging welcome in the next. A village man bought a Bible and served us tea. He said he listened to a Christian radio broadcast and believed the gospel, but he didn't dare tell his family or relatives."

"Why not? I should think he would want to."

"It might mean ostracism, loss of his job, poison in his coffee or ground glass in his food. Muslim persecution is usually inevitable. Converts to Christianity are considered heretics and must be annihilated."

"Now I understand what the term, 'secret believer' means."

"Yes. That great missionary medical doctor, Samuel

Zwemer, who worked in Saudi Arabia in a Dutch Reformed Mission hospital, said that he believed many Christians would rise from Muslim graves in the resurrection!"

"What a great day that will be! Won't we all be happily surprised at meeting so many brave souls in heaven!"

"Someone told me that the Muslims say, 'When we finish with Saturday, we'll start on Sunday.' It means, when they finally exterminate the Jews, they will begin on the Christians. They have vowed to rule the world. We need to pray for our enemies."

"I agree. Tell me about more of your happier experiences."

"I think the work I loved most was what you may have guessed already. Our project was 'Bibles for Bedouins-- a Bible in Every Tent.' We visited in their tents and became their friends. In fifteen years we distributed hundreds of Arabic Bibles and I believe God's Word will produce results. Only His Holy Spirit can convict, convince and convert their hearts."

"I agree. Was that your only job? I think not. You probably wore many hats."

"I taught a Bible class at an International Christian School in Jerusalem for twelve years."

"Tell me about it."

"There were children from all over the world: Russia, England, Scotland, Ireland, South America, India, Africa, North America, the Fiji Islands, Canada. Their parents were with various religious groups, the United Nations, in business or various jobs."

"What level did you teach?"

"The first few years there were as many as sixty-five children in first, second and third grades. Then the headmaster divided the classes. Another missionary took the older children and I kept first grade only, with an average of eighteen."

"I assume you adapted your lessons for such a diversity of ethnic backgrounds?"

"Yes. I developed my own curriculum and kept it simple so that the children who spoke very little English could understand. They picked up the language quickly, and soon they were chattering with their friends. Children are amazingly adaptable."

"What kinds of lessons did you use?"

"I started with the Wordless Book and correlated each Bible story with a filmstrip. The Jungle Doctor Series fascinated the children."

"How did they respond?"

"They loved the analogies of monkeys learning to obey their parents, avoiding danger, making friends, honoring the advice of their elders and getting into trouble when they disobeyed.

"One of my most effective tools was a simplified illustrated version of 'Pilgrim's Progress.' Whenever I read the chapter of how Pilgrim's burden fell off at the cross and rolled down the hill, I regularly gave an invitation. Several children always responded and stayed after school to pray.

"During the twelve years that I taught, approximately two hundred children accepted Jesus as their Savior. It was heartwarming to mark a little red cross beside their names in my record book. I still pray for them."

"I know what you mean. When I saw some of our young seminary students grow in their spiritual walk with God, and unconditionally commit their lives to Him for His service, I walked on cloud nine! Like you, I pray for the young people who have made that momentous decision."

Abby was reluctant to end this very pleasant and special conversation. "There are lots of stories we could share but it's late and we have another long day ahead of us tomorrow. Good night, Peter, and pleasant dreams."

"And to you, Abby. God bless you with joy." Peter stood as she left, then sat down to think. *Abby is a very special lady. The Lord has brought her into my life for a particular reason. I treasure every moment we spend together. I wonder if she feels the same way?*

Chapter 10

Solomon's Bay

At dawn Abby woke up everyone to watch a magnificent sunrise. Sure enough, the water of the Red Sea was glowing a deep crimson that slowly turned bright and then blended into shining pink and gold as the sun rose higher.

Sam brought the van and Abby urged her friends to come immediately. "I thought you might like having breakfast at an oasis along the sea."

"What? No breakfast now? I cannot possibly wait that long. Chalk up another miss for Abby," grouched Lisa. "What are you going to subject us to today?"

Colin decided it was his turn again to defend Abby. "Stop it, Lisa. We've had enough of your incessant criticism. We're not going to permit your negative attitude to spoil our vacation. It's the best one we've ever had. Quit putting down Abby. She's doing a superb job and we'll never be able to repay her. If you don't like what we're doing, have the courtesy to keep quiet. Some day you'll regret your unkind remarks and have to ask forgiveness. I guarantee it. I know from experience."

"Apologize? Never!" Lisa replied emphatically. But Colin's strong reprimand proved effective, for a short time at least, because the woman was quiet for the rest of the morning.

As the group drove along the sea, Megan stared at the stony mountains on their right. "Oh, those glorious colors: orange, pink, rusty-red, green, turquoise, blue! Some of them resemble marble cakes, swirled with vanilla and chocolate. Others are striped and staggered in layers like stair steps. They looked dull gray last night. Now they're breathtaking."

"It's the way the sun reflects on the rock," Colin stated. "You're quite right, love. I hope this camera will catch those shades of color."

"God uses a unique paintbrush, doesn't He!" Peter added.

Abby pointed to an unusual oblong island. "Those odd shapes you see sticking up are the ruins of a castle that must have been enchanting. There is a natural pool along its shore. Pirates used to hide there and loot ships sailing up the gulf to deposit their booty. They were an easy prey."

"Our children would love to explore there, wouldn't they, Colin?"

"They're not the only ones," he laughed. "We'll just have to come back as a family."

"All those stones up the valley look blue and pink. There must be thousands. I've never seen so many like that," Megan observed.

Beneath a palm tree beside the sea they had a 'continental' breakfast of delicious sweet rolls, fruit and coffee the hotel had furnished. Abby gazed across the water and softly quoted, "'When you pass through the water, I will be with you.'"

Turning to Lisa, she said, "You missed our discussion last night. Peter, would you mind repeating what you told us?"

"That promise," Peter said, "means that whatever our problem or circumstances, we have God's assurance that He is with us like He was with Moses. Nothing happens in our lives that He does not permit for our good and His glory."

"Are you certain of that?" asked Lisa as she looked closely into his face.

"Absolutely."

"Then why did my stupid husband leave me?" Her voice was defiant and her face flushed with anger.

Solomon's Bay

"I cannot answer that. But if you ask the Lord, He might show you."

Lisa made no reply. She scowled and turned to look out across the sea.

Abby was stunned. She had assumed Lisa was a widow because her behavior seemed inappropriate for a married woman. Lisa had not mentioned a husband. But then she had never discussed her personal life with any of her friends. She certainly had not given the impression that she was a chronic faultfinder. *No matter. In spite of her apparent wealth, the poor woman is unhappy and needs all the help we can give her. The Lord had a good reason for causing her to join this tour. I must show her His loving kindness by example.* Again Abby prayed for God to give her patience and understanding.

The water was clear and inviting, and they put on their swimsuits. Lisa looked extremely attractive as she paraded up and down, glancing toward Peter occasionally to make sure he was watching. Colin blew air into a big beach ball Abby produced and they played an exhilarating game.

Camels grazed nearby. "Look at that baby staying close to its mother," Megan said. "Oh, something must have frightened them. How funny they look, running like that!" Their crooked legs splayed outward and their thick lips loosely flapped up and down! The couples laughed hilariously and Abby and Peter joined in. Lisa ignored the spectacle, frowning her disgust.

After they dressed and were ready to leave, several young Bedouin boys from a nearby camp came along. They spied the baby camel and began to chase it. It scampered here and there until they cornered it in some bushes. As they closed in, the little animal opened its mouth and spewed out a stream of ugly green liquid that sprayed all over them!

"Maybe they deserve that for frightening the poor little thing," chuckled Andrew.

"I thought I'd like to join in the fun, but not with that kind of a reward!" Colin added.

Comforting Arms

Megan heartily agreed. "I'm not sure I want to ride one, either. It looked like it might be bumpy when they trot or run."

"Some historians say this is the place where King Solomon's ships brought gold, silver, ivory, apes and peacocks. We saw Solomon's Pools near Bethlehem, Solomon's Pillars yesterday and now this charming oasis called Solomon's Bay. There are also Solomon's Quarries and his Stables in Jerusalem."

"He was quite a guy," Colin said with admiration. "Wise, rich and probably handsome, considering all the wives and concubines he had, as well as lots of children, undoubtedly."

"But oh, those women. How they got him into trouble!" Andrew added.

"Enough said. Stop right there!" demanded Megan, laughing.

With a pleasant grin, Peter said, "Andrew was probably thinking of how Solomon's wives led him astray. He turned to other gods and even built a place for pagan worship. Rather thankless behavior after God had blessed him with wisdom and riches."

Andrew asked Peter to videotape Cindy and himself with the sea in the background and palm trees beside them. "This will be the perfect reminder of our time spent here," he said lovingly as he put his arm around her. "Come and join us, everyone."

Farther inland were breathtaking views of jagged stony peaks cleanly outlined against bright sky and snowy clouds. At the base of the mountains blue and green stones were strewn among tumbleweed and scraggly acacia trees.

Several huts of a Bedouin camp appeared at the end of a rocky valley. Sam drove as far as he could and parked. Abby led the team over the stones to a group of men squatting on the ground. Their camels were hobbled close by. True to custom, they quickly spread old quilts on the ground and graciously invited the guests to sit down.

Solomon's Bay

"Look at this magnificent scene!" Peter said, and Abby translated so the men would know what he was saying. "Camels stand in bold relief against the blue sky and beyond is the deeper blue of the sea. Here and there bends a lone palm tree. It's an artist's delight!"

Bedouins with their camels ambled toward a tank of fresh water a few hundred feet away. "How do you find enough food and water for your animals in this arid country?" Andrew asked.

"We save the rainwater in winter, and where you find palm trees there usually is fresh water available. The animals survive on what they can scrounge from trees and bushes. Sometimes we bring in bales of hay or a tank of water like you see there."

A goat's two newborn kids played beside a woman who was preparing food nearby. The narrow red and black satin band wrapped around her forehead was fastened with strips of cloth covered with coins that streamed down in front of her eyes, nose and cheeks. Her dress was ragged. Two chubby children clung to her skirt, their big black eyes peeking shyly at the strangers. Over a small fire of twigs on the sand she cooked sweet wheat pancakes, smeared them with goat fat and sprinkled them with sugar. One of the men served them to the guests.

"These are delicious. Thank you, "Abby said, and she made excuses for Lisa's turned-up nose of refusal.

Next the woman placed a pot of tea on a metal holder over the fire. When it was ready, again one of the men served. Abby was glad the others were good sports even though they could see the glasses were not clean and neither were the hands that had prepared the drink.

She offered the men Bibles from her supply and said, "This is the Word of God. The Koran says every good Muslim should be reading it because it contains the five books of Moses, the Psalms of David and the life of the Messiah."

The men readily accepted the books. "I'm a teacher.

I'll read out loud so the rest can hear," one of them said. Another disappeared and came back with thick round chunks of dried yogurt that he presented to Abby. She thanked them for their gracious hospitality. "Now it's time to go on. If all goes well, we should get to Mt. Sinai tonight."

In the van, Lisa bombarded Abby with criticism. "How can I endure this constant humiliation? I feel absolutely dirty from sitting on those raggedy quilts. There's sand in my shoes. I'm extremely uncomfortable. You know I have a delicate digestive system and I have to refuse eating or drinking with those people. Situations like these are absolutely abhorrent. Why do you continue to drag us into them, Abby? Why do you persist in subjecting me to such treatment? Answer me. No, don't. You do it on purpose just to mortify me. You don't know how terrible I feel."

"I'm sorry, Lisa. I'll try to be more considerate from now on."

"But I love these experiences, Abby," Megan said. "Next time, let Lisa stay in the van. Don't deprive us of enjoying such unique treats."

"I agree," Andrew said. "Lisa, you need to remember that the rest of us should be considered. It's not everyone who gets a chance to see and experience such special treatment among tribes who are little known by many people in the world. We are privileged to have this personal touch on our tour."

"It's purely personal, as far as I'm concerned," Lisa spit out. "Abby thinks only of herself and what she likes to do. She does not consider my comfort or preferences, only her own. I'm sorry I ever came."

"That's enough said, Lisa. You're actually blaming Abby for your own faults. Why don't you try being a good sport and cut out the sarcasm. Let's change the subject, shall we?" Colin said firmly. "I'm anxious to see what's around the next curve of these fantastic mountains. We're really isolated in this vast deserted wilderness. In three hours we've only seen one truck pass us."

Solomon's Bay

"How about a song or two while we travel?" Peter suggested. "Do you know 'What a Friend We Have in Jesus'?"

"That's a great idea. Thank you, Peter. Our Arab youth group always sang while we traveled. Will you lead us? Perhaps we'll discover that we have a choir with soprano, alto, tenor and bass. We can 'make beautiful music together'!"

They laughed and began singing, each joining in until lovely harmony developed. Lisa did not cooperate and was the only sullen passenger. "How much longer until we get to where we're going?" she interrupted.

"Oh, Lisa, you sound just like our children when we travel!" Megan giggled. "We'll be there in good time, I'm sure."

"Not soon enough for me. I hope the hotel is air-conditioned. I cannot stand this terrible heat much longer. It's a good thing this van is cool or I would simply melt."

"We'll be staying in St. Catherine's monastery. I doubt if there is air-conditioning but these mountains cool off considerably at night and you may even need a light blanket. That should enable you to get a good night's sleep."

"It had better, or I won't be fit to live with tomorrow."

Abby wanted to retort, *You aren't, anyway. I can understand why your husband left you. He wasn't so stupid after all!*

Chapter 11

Mt. Sinai

Sam turned the van away from the Red Sea into the mountains. Clouds streaked the deep blue sky. The road leveled out into a valley filled with all kinds of oddly shaped stone formations.

"Monsters! That's what they look like," exclaimed Megan.

"You're right, they do have funny shapes," Colin agreed.

"Yes," Abby said, "it's because over the years, powerful desert winds blow sand against the big chunks of limestone and slowly gouge away soft parts. It's the process of erosion."

"There's a dragon, and a fort," Cindy said.

"I see a castle, a big turtle and some giant-size mushrooms," added Andrew.

"Look! An ape...a lizard...a haystack and some people profiles. I wonder what Joe and Gina would say about this?" Megan murmured.

"And a palace and some logs. They'd love it!" Colin answered.

"You people have wild imaginations," snickered Lisa. "You act more like children than adults. You ought to be ashamed of yourselves."

Her cynicism was ignored.

Bedouin camps were few and far between. Goats grazed on tufts of grass and scrubby bushes. Camels nibbled on thorny acacia trees. "The animals all belong to Bedouins

Mt. Sinai

and if you look carefully, you'll find someone is tending them. Do you see those odd bags fastened to ropes hanging from the tree branches? They belong to Bedouins who store their supplies that way, out of reach of marauders."

"Where do the animals get enough food to eat in these stony mountains and this sandy desert?" asked Megan.

"There are bushes and trees in some places, and oases in the mountains. Whenever it rains, new grass springs up automatically and beautiful wildflowers in a variety of colors carpet some of the deserts," Abby said. "Even bright scarlet tulips pop up in unexpected places. Arabs believe anemones are 'the lilies of the field' Jesus described when He said, 'Solomon in all his glory was not arrayed like one of these.'

"On Fridays the city markets and street corners are filled with lots of specially grown flowers for sale. The Jews use them to decorate their tables for the Sabbath. Israel exports a variety of flowers to Europe. They're grown in a kibbutz, a farm where many people live and work together to grow or produce things like grain, dairy products, fruit, vegetables, candles and clothes."

They stopped at a little Bedouin shop made of palm branches, and Abby ordered tea. As usual, it was sweet and flavored with mint.

"No ice here, I suppose," Lisa groaned. "Count me out. I'm hot enough."

"It's delicious and refreshing, Lisa. Try it."

No response.

They drove on. The sun beat down intensely. Great gusts of wind whirled dust devils and rolled tumbleweeds somersaulting pell-mell across the road. Sand blown against the mountains had formed giant slides like ski slopes.

"Wouldn't our children have fun sliding down that huge sand pile!" Megan said. "I can just see them climbing up and down. It would release their pent-up energy."

"You're right," Colin agreed, "and I might even join them!"

After nearly four hours of traveling eighty miles

Comforting Arms

inland on rough, stony tracks, Abby said, "St. Catherine's Monastery is up ahead at the foot of Mt. Sinai. The monks spend their whole life there in seclusion, tending the garden, cooking, serving, cleaning and performing various duties. I've reserved rooms for two nights. We'll need to leave early in the morning while it's cool enough to climb the mountain comfortably. I'm sure you all are ready to have a good meal and relax."

"I should hope so. It's about time!" was Lisa's comment. After a simple but adequate dinner of rice and vegetables, she hurried to her room but she could not sleep. She tossed and turned. Suddenly she jumped out of bed and screamed frantically. Abby, followed by Andrew, burst through the door and tried to calm her.

"What's wrong? A bad dream? Are you sick? How can we help you?" Andrew asked.

"What was that terrible noise I just heard? There it is again!"

"It sounded like a wildcat. I saw a badger, a jackal and some donkeys nosing around the garbage cans when I took a walk outside," Andrew said.

"Oh. So now we're in this isolated country where there are wild animals roaming around! What have you gotten us into this time, Abby?"

"Don't worry, Lisa. Tourists come here constantly and as far as I know, no one has ever been injured. The government would not want that to happen."

"Of course not. They would lose business and that involves money," she retorted. "Well, at least we're inside where it's safe." She breathed a big sigh of relief. "But what about tomorrow?" She frowned. "I'm not sure I want to go, with danger like that lurking who knows where. I think I'll stay here."

"It will be all right. Those animals prowl around at night and sleep in the daytime. We'll be fine. The Lord will watch over us. We've several strong men to protect us, too. Now have a good rest and don't worry."

Mt. Sinai

Protesting about lack of sleep and the dangers they faced, Lisa was late joining the group an hour before dawn the next morning. After drinking a cup of stimulating hot tea, they started climbing the path to the top of the mountain, using flashlights to pierce the darkness. It was rough with pebbles and stones. Lisa insisted that Peter walk beside her and she clutched his arm tenaciously.

The sun rose in soft shades of pink and orange, outlining the mountain peaks. They all stood quietly for a few minutes, watching the miracle. Softly, Peter prayed and thanked God for another day, closing with His comforting promise, "As I was with Moses, so I will be with thee..."

The climbers soon felt warm enough to shed their light jackets. They passed an oasis where Bedouins were living, surrounded by palm trees, grass and bushes. Farther along were huge rocks and enormous boulders. A gigantic one was split down the middle. The path led through the wide split where the sun had not penetrated. It was cool and shady. They had been climbing for two hours so while they stood there to rest, Abby began to hum a tune. "We sing about this in church, 'He hideth my soul in the cleft of the rock.'"

"Now I understand what that means," said Cindy. "It feels good to get away from that hot sun. And Jesus is our Rock! That's like another hymn we know, 'Jesus is a Rock in a weary land.' Isn't God good to provide this shade for needy mountain climbers!"

They pushed on, winding upward. The trail appeared endless. "I'm completely exhausted," gasped Lisa. "How much farther do we have to go? I've got to rest." She plopped down onto a rock and refused to budge. "We've been climbing nearly four hours. We'll never reach the top. It's just too far."

"It's only a short distance now. Try to make it. We can rest when we get there. Look at that fantastic view of the mountains below us. We're higher than all the others, and closer to heaven! Maybe that's why God chose this particular mountain. It's a breathtaking sight!"

"It's breathtaking, all right," Lisa agreed sarcastically. "Mine is absolutely gone."

Peter gently took Lisa's arm to help her up, and reluctantly she slowly got to her feet. Clinging to him for support, she stumbled along, panting.

Abruptly, at the top of steep stone steps, they found a large flat area. A little chapel stood on one side, but it was locked. Nearby was a small room with an open door. They went in and sat in a circle on the floor to recover and eat the sandwiches and fruit in their backpacks.

"How high are we?" asked Colin.

"Eight thousand feet," answered Abby.

"There's less oxygen here. That's why we had a hard time breathing during the last part of the climb," Andrew explained.

"I wonder if Moses got out of breath when he climbed up here?" mused Megan.

"No doubt he did. Peter, would you read the Ten Commandments?" Abby handed him a small Bible.

"'Thou shalt have no other gods before me.

Thou shalt not make unto thee any graven image.

Thou shalt not take the name of the Lord thy God in vain.

Remember the sabbath day, to keep it holy.

Honour thy father and thy mother.

Thou shalt not kill.

Thou shalt not commit adultery.

Thou shalt not steal.

Thou shalt not bear false witness.

Thou shalt not covet.'"

They sang a few hymns, Peter led in prayer and then they began the long trek down.

"I simply cannot do this," Lisa said. "My legs are like jelly. This is an impossible situation, Abby. Couldn't you have arranged a ride for us? There must be some other way to get down. I refuse to budge another inch."

Mt. Sinai

She dropped down on a rock and the determined look on her face convinced Abby she needed to find help. *"Oh Lord,"* she quietly breathed, *"please in some way relieve this situation. You are the God of miracles. I come to You."*

Before she finished praying, several Bedouins approached leading camels. Abby was stunned by this sudden immediate display of God's provision. She asked if they would let her friends ride. Megan and Cindy were relieved because their legs were getting wobbly, too. There were four animals so Abby was able to ride as well.

Megan giggled as the clumsy camels knelt at their owners' command. The kind Bedouins gently helped each of the ladies up to the wooden saddle fastened onto the top of the hump. Even Lisa did not object to this means of relief, though she had trouble climbing onto the kneeling animal and called for Peter's assistance.

Abby warned them, "Hold on tightly, now."

Megan and Cindy quickly grabbed hold of their saddle horns and clung desperately as the animals stood up with three violent jerks. They felt as if they were going to slide right down the long neck, then in the opposite direction off the tail! Lisa screamed, threw her hands up in the air and jumped to the ground. "No! I can't do this!" she wailed.

"Just try again," Abby urged. "It's the only way you can get down the mountain if you don't want to walk."

"Peter, help me," Lisa begged. He boosted her up again and she hurriedly grabbed the saddle horn and held on desperately. Her face was tense with fear and misery as she was jerked back and forth, then she felt relief as the animal began to move forward steadily. Even Cindy was frightened at first, but as they rocked along she soon decided this was the way to go!

"God certainly supplied our need for help to get down this mountain," Megan said cheerily.

"That He did," Abby agreed. "I was praying and before I finished, God answered. He does things like that!"

Three Bedouin girls guarded their goats a short

Comforting Arms

distance away. Chattering in Arabic, they greeted the travelers. Abby translated, "They want to know if you would like to take their picture."

"By all means," Colin replied as he prepared to focus.

Each girl promptly removed a bag that hung down her back. The bags were woven from thick colored yarn and fastened to a cord wound around the girl's head. They opened their 'purses' and took out precious treasures: wide belts decorated with tiny brightly colored beads, and headdresses of cowry shells that were used as money for trading a long time ago. They put on their ornaments and posed for the picture. To thank them, Abby gave each one a few cookies, dates and gospels of John. The girls smiled in appreciation.

When the group arrived at the monastery, Abby repeated the warning to hold on because again there would be two violent jerks as each camel knelt. This time they were prepared and Megan and Cindy laughed with pleasure as they climbed down. Lisa looked disheveled and disgusted. Colin, Andrew and Peter shook hands with the men, paid them and thanked them for their help.

It was late afternoon. Abby had arranged a brief tour of the fortress-like monastery. A guide told them that in the third century, Christian refugees fled from Roman persecution and sought safety there. Later came hermits who built a chapel on the summit. St. Catherine's was founded in 527 by a Byzantine emperor named Justinian, who dedicated it to his consort, Theodora. The area was walled for protection because desert nomads occasionally harassed and even murdered the Greek Orthodox monks residing there. About a dozen monks still carry on the work. At night the gates are closed.

The name St. Catherine commemorates a royal virgin from Egypt who was converted to Christianity and martyred in Alexandria. Three hundred years later a monk dreamed he would find a treasure on the mountain. He discovered the

Mt. Sinai

body of St. Katherine who had been carried there by flights of angels!

The guide showed them the library containing three thousand four hundred manuscripts, a world-famous collection of two thousand icons, courtyards, cells and workshops and the massive Church of the Transfiguration. Its centerpiece was a mosaic showing Jesus with Moses and Elijah. In front of the altar was a marble stand holding two golden caskets containing St. Katherine's head and part of an arm. Her relics are carried through the monastery in a solemn procession annually.

Near the walls they saw a small whitewashed building known as the Charnel House. A hermit who died keeps silent watch by candlelight. His skeleton is dressed in a purple monastic cowl and cloak. A rosary and staff are in his hand. Two vaulted rooms hold the bones of all the monks who have died in the monastery. Their bodies are buried in a tiny cemetery and later the fleshless remains are exhumed and deposited in one of the rooms according to the monastic hierarchy. Bishops are placed separately in individually named niches. The rest are piled in heaps of skulls, arms, hands, and feet.

After the tour the group sat down to another frugal dinner of rice and vegetables, and then they gathered in the tiny guest lounge. Again, Lisa disappeared before they began devotions. It had been a long tiring day and they all were more than ready for a good night's sleep.

The next morning they started back to the town of Elat. The mountains appeared more spectacular at each turn of the road. "Our Joe would be counting every camel, and little Gina would be numbering the goats near these Bedouin camps," mused Megan.

The sea glittered temptingly and Sam pulled into an oasis shaded by palm trees.

"How about another swim?" Abby suggested.

"Yes, let's," responded Megan exuberantly.

The women changed in the van, men outside. The

water shimmered in varied shades of light green, turquoise, deep blue and purple. Near the shore it was so clear they could see the bottom. They were careful not to step on sharp coral or spiny black sea urchins. The moment Lisa saw one she screamed and dashed madly for the shore. "No more swimming for me," she groaned, gritting her teeth angrily.

For the remainder of the return trip, they followed a different route. Abby explained, "We're going to see an unusual crater. It's a wide, deep area in the earth where scientists believe a giant meteor fell from the sky many years ago. Now there's a road through it."

"Surprise!" exclaimed Abby as they drove along. "Look at the wildflowers blooming. Aren't they pretty? It must have rained here."

Only Peter answered, "Yes. Incredible acres of beauty."

Abby looked around and was surprised to see the rest of the travelers asleep.

"It's been an exceptional trip," Peter said, "filled with cherished experiences for all of us. Thank you, Abby."

Chapter 12

Joppa

After the trip to Sinai Abby planned a leisurely day. "We're going to Jaffa, the new Jewish name for the old city of Joppa, then on to Caesarea for a swim in the Mediterranean Sea. So tuck bathing suits, towels and extra clothes into your bags and we'll be on our way," Abby advised.

"It's about time," Lisa grumbled softly so that only Abby could hear.

Beyond Jerusalem, fields of grain were ripening in the warm sun. "We're driving through the valley of Ajalon. Peter, would you remind us of what happened here?"

"Yes. Joshua and his army were fighting their enemies and to give them more time, God made the sun and moon stand still for a whole day. He caused the enemies to be frightened and as they retreated, He sent huge hailstones crashing down on them. It took Joshua and his men that whole extra day to finish the battle."

"Why were they enemies? Why did they have to be destroyed?" asked Megan.

"Because they worshipped idols and not the true living God," Andrew answered.

"Those people were breaking the very first commandment God gave to Moses, that only He should be worshipped," added Cindy.

"You're both quite right," commented Peter as the car sped along the highway. "God must punish sin. That's a basic rule of theology."

"I don't agree. Sometimes He punishes us for no reason at all!" Lisa said bitterly. "I haven't done anything to deserve what I've been through. It's not fair!"

"God always has a good reason for what He permits to happen to us. It may be to teach us a lesson or to strengthen our faith or in order that we may help someone who has the same problem."

"Well, if you say so. But I'm not convinced."

"Sam, we've time to stop at Emmaus." They walked among the ruins and Abby reminded them that after His death and resurrection, Jesus walked there from Jerusalem and talked to the two disciples who were discussing the events of the day. "What they said to the disciples when they returned to Jerusalem is the same phrase we use at Easter, 'The Lord is risen!'"

"I love that!" Cindy said reverently. "This is a beautiful spot for remembering."

"We'll have more opportunities to do that, especially since we'll be in Jerusalem to celebrate Easter."

"I can hardly wait!" Megan's face glowed. "This is the most wonderful trip we've ever taken. Right, Colin?"

"Right, my love."

"Well, now that we've seen it, let's get on with it. I'm anxious for a swim," Lisa urged.

From a distance, dark clouds of pollution hovered over the metropolis of Tel Aviv. Sam got lost hunting for a road leading to Joppa, and they drove around in circles, ending up several times at a tall clock tower.

"I'd think you could direct the driver so we wouldn't have to go around Robin Hood's barn trying to find the proper road. This route should have been mapped out and discussed with Sam beforehand," Lisa accused, as she turned to face Abby. "What a wretched tour guide you've turned out to be."

This time, Peter defended Abby. "That's enough, Lisa. Stop your unwelcome abusive harangues. We've had more than enough of them. Anyone could lose their way in this maze of streets, let alone heavy traffic."

Abby felt embarrassed, but at the same time relieved by Peter's defense. And by this time she knew any apology, however sincere, would not be accepted. Yet she felt one was in order and offered it humbly. "I'm sorry, Lisa. We're doing our best. We always have trouble here because Tel Aviv is Israel's largest city and it's spread out to include Joppa. It's difficult to negotiate these complicated streets. They're very old and they turn and twist without rhyme or reason."

"We understand," consoled Cindy.

Sam made another turn, the right one this time, and drove until he found a comfortable place for them to sit and look out over the Mediterranean Sea.

"Just think," Megan exclaimed, "we're in Joppa where Jonah tried to run away from God because he didn't want to go to Nineveh."

A ship outlined on the horizon slowly disappeared. Megan continued the story. "I wonder how far he swam before he got swallowed by that big fish?"

"And as a result, Jonah was glad to obey God," finished Peter. "He learned obedience the hard way."

"Sometimes we're like that, aren't we?" Cindy said. "We prefer our own way instead of God's."

Lisa's expression hardened and Abby surmised that selfishness probably was the cause of the woman's problems. *But who am I to judge? Only God knows what is in her heart and why she seems so bitter.*

Peter continued, "But His plan for our lives is a thousand times better than we ever could imagine. If we let Him, He will guide us in every decision we make."

"Well, I make my own decisions," Lisa snapped. "No one else is going to make them for me, I can assure you of that. What does God care about the problems we have? He's got bigger things to worry about in this wicked world."

"Lisa, I assure you, He *is* concerned about everything we do. He just wants us to let Him have control of our lives."

Comforting Arms

She ignored Peter's remark and turned to look out over the water.

"Joppa was an important Crusader stronghold but Napoleon razed it in 1799. Now it houses Arabs. In fact, my friends live here. Would you like to visit them for a few minutes?"

"Yes," Cindy and Megan said enthusiastically. The men agreed.

Lisa was silent. Then she spoke up, "Here we go again! Not another tent, I hope?"

"Sam, turn here. It's just down the street. We can't stay long but I'm sure you would enjoy meeting them."

The house was small but the welcome was warm. A gracious woman greeted Abby with a kiss on each cheek. "Friends, meet Lily, an Arab Christian."

"My husband is at work. George," she motioned to one of the children, "go and call him. He won't want to miss seeing you. Please sit down. I'll make coffee."

Without thinking, Lisa spoke her mind. "Oh, no. Not again. I can't stand the stuff. It's disgusting. How the rest of you can possibly drink it is beyond me. It tastes like bitter medicine. You won't sleep tonight, I assure you." She tossed back her long hair to emphasize her remarks.

Abby was both embarrassed and shocked at the thoughtless outburst and hurriedly explained that Lisa was unable to tolerate coffee.

"I understand," Lily responded. "Would you like a soft drink instead? I'll send for some."

"No thank you," Abby said. "We can't stay long. I just wanted my friends to meet some of our Christian Arabs. Here's Adnan."

He welcomed Abby enthusiastically and insisted they stay for lunch.

"I'm sorry, we can't. We're on our way to Caesarea. How is the church progressing? Tell us about your work."

"We're growing. Young people are coming in response to our advertising, and they're inviting their friends, who in turn invite their peers as well as their parents. Whole families are being baptized. We can never thank you and your husband enough for coming every week to hold that Bible study in our home. Now we have more than fifty attending the chapel we've built."

"That's good news, Adnan. I'm glad to hear it. Peter, here, is a seminary professor."

"Where did you train for the ministry?" Peter asked.

"I went to the States and studied in New York. Those were hard years but they were worth it. Would you have time to come and speak for us while you are here?"

"I'd love to do that but it depends upon the schedule Abby has for us."

"Perhaps after the tour ends we can arrange it," Abby suggested.

"Good. Let us know when it's convenient. We'll come to escort you."

"That's kind of you," Abby replied. "We'll keep in touch. Now we need to go on. Thank you for the coffee and sweets, Lily."

The sea was a bright blue with gently rolling waves. Windsurfers with their colorful sails gave way to fishing boats farther up the coast. As they drove along, Abby handed out carrot sticks and raisins for a healthy snack. Even Lisa couldn't object to this, she thought.

But she was wrong. "Are we children, that you have to give us this kind of fare?" she asked. "It's nearly lunch time, anyway. Have you forgotten?"

"No, I haven't. But we'll be in Caesarea soon and we can eat on the beach. It's lovely there."

Chapter 13

Caesarea

The journey from Joppa along the Mediterranean seacoast took the travelers past the city of Netanya, where brides and grooms on their honeymoon were given rides in fancy decorated horse-and-buggy carriages. After another half-hour they reached the outskirts of Caesarea and found a parking area close to the sea.

As soon as the van stopped, everyone hurried to change into swimsuits and head for the water. "Please wait until you see which flag is flying," Abby advised. "A red one warns that it's dangerous to swim; a black one means no swimming at all. Oh, the sea looks calm and the white flag is waving. That means it's safe to go in. I'll have lunch ready as soon as you've had enough."

They splashed in the water and played catch with a beach ball. A lifeguard was stationed nearby. Lisa took one look at him, quickly dove into the water and swam far out. Then she waved her arms and screamed for help. Peter and the lifeguard instantly jumped in and they both reached her at the same time. Peter fell back to let the guard control the situation.

The rescue was quick, and the guard carried Lisa to shore. He scolded her vehemently, warning her to keep within safe bounds. She smiled and said, "Of course. I didn't realize I was out so far. I'm terribly sorry." She gazed at the handsome man admiringly, her big blue eyes wide and sparkling. He promptly dropped her onto the sand and walked away without a backward glance.

He seems disgusted with women who employ tricks like that, Abby thought. *I'm embarrassed but I guess I should be used to her behavior by now. Help me to be forgiving, patient and understanding, Lord.*

When they relaxed on quilts to eat lunch, Abby asked, "What does that lifeguard remind you of?"

Megan quickly responded, "Our guardian angel who watches over us?"

"A good idea. What happens if you disobey the rules?"

"It could mean danger or even death."

"What a lesson for us to remember! I like the way you draw a spiritual application from these places we visit, Abby. I appreciate your keen insight."

"Thank you, Colin. Do you remember the airport where we landed?"

"Yes. There were planes from many countries of the world."

"That place is called Lod. In Bible times the name was Lydda and it's near here. Let's take turns reading from the book of Acts. We'll be reminded and perhaps surprised at all of the exciting things that happened in this area."

"Whew!" Megan exclaimed, "We read more than one story. First, about..." she turned back the page, "Aeneas in Lydda. Peter prayed and Jesus healed him."

"Then Dorcas in Joppa," added Cindy. "She was raised from the dead!"

Colin continued, "Next was the Roman soldier Cornelius in Caesarea, right here where we are! What wonderful miracles!"

"Through Peter, Jesus healed the sick, raised the dead and answered prayer. God did this so that many of the people might believe and glorify Him," Peter added.

"You've summed it up perfectly," Abby said. "Now let's have another swim."

It was late afternoon when they packed the picnic basket and folded the quilts. Abby pointed to a long brick building. "Over there is where the apostle Paul was put in prison by his enemies before he appealed to Caesar and was sent to Rome."

"He was shipwrecked on the way," Andrew added.

"Yes, but an angel appeared to him and said, 'Do not be afraid.' He promised Paul that everyone on the ship would be saved and they were. God keeps His promises, doesn't He?" Peter said.

"And His promises are for us to claim, too!" Abby added.

"Right. As we claim them for ourselves we grow in faith, and we experience His hand at work in our lives."

"That's clear thinking, Peter," Colin responded. "I've tried it, and I know it works."

"While we're here we should visit the Roman amphitheater where early Christians probably were forced to fight gladiators or lions."

"Gladiators and lions? Let's go!" Colin and Andrew were ready to investigate.

"Ugh," was Lisa's response. She trudged behind as they filed into the arena and scanned the semicircle rows of stone seats.

"This is like the large one in Rome where Christians were tortured and burned at the stake," Cindy observed.

"I wonder what was down here?" Megan stooped to look through an iron grating. Underneath was a dark hole. "Could this have been a lion's den?"

"Or a dungeon?" Colin got down on his hands and knees to peer into the blackness. The idea piqued his imagination.

Cindy climbed up the steps and sat down on one of the seats beside Lisa. She was thinking about what gruesome events might have occurred as entertainment hundreds of years ago. She remembered her visit to Italy and the awesome things she had seen in Rome.

"Lisa, did you ever tramp through the catacombs?"

"I certainly did not. I had no desire to see those

terrible underground passages and caves where early Christians hid to escape persecution or murder by their enemies."

"We saw graves hollowed out of stone where the dead were placed. And we sat on the steps of the huge coliseum and talked about martyrs who bravely fought gladiators and lions, or were burned at the stake rather than renounce their faith in Christ. We even noticed a small cross carved into a stone near the entrance where a Christian had left his parting testimony."

"I don't know why I came on this tour," Lisa said despondently. "I'm tired and disgusted. But it seemed like a good idea to get away from my troubles. It hasn't worked, though. I brought them with me. How are you always so cheerful?"

"I've learned to let Jesus take over my problems. He can solve them better than I can. In their place, He gives me comfort and peace."

"Peace! That's something I don't have. Maybe I'll find it while I'm here."

"I'll pray that you will," Cindy replied, and gently patted Lisa's arm. "Would you like to talk about your problems?"

"No. Not yet. It's a hopeless situation. No one can help."

As they all walked back to the car, Megan asked, "Why did God permit people to persecute the Christians?"

"The majority of the Romans and Jews did not believe Jesus was their Savior," Peter answered. "They thought the Christians were trying to overthrow the government to establish their own kingdom. Jesus' message was about a heavenly kingdom. They didn't understand that He came to give men peace in their hearts."

Abby continued, "Perhaps God also permitted persecution so that the Christians would be scattered to other countries, and from the testimony of their lives the gospel would be spread. This is still happening in some parts of the world. Later on we'll see a place where Christians hid to avoid persecution," Abby promised. "Now it's dinner time. Let's head for our hotel."

After the meal Peter led devotions in a secluded lounge. "We've been talking about promises today. Why don't we each repeat a special promise and tell why it is meaningful. Abby, would you start us off?"

"Alright. When I was a young girl of fourteen I knew in my heart that God wanted me to be a missionary. But I didn't know how to tell people about Jesus. One morning I felt really concerned about it. I pulled a little card from a box of 'Promises' my mother kept on the kitchen table. It read, 'Now therefore go, and I will be with thy mouth, and teach thee what thou shalt say.' I looked up the verse in the Bible and learned that God was talking to Moses. It fit my need. I believed God would honor His promise, and He did! I studied the basics of evangelism when I attended Bible College. While my husband attended seminary I took a course in Child Evangelism and learned how to use the Wordless Book. That was exactly the training I needed because my whole missionary career has involved telling people about Jesus."

"Who'll be next?"

Andrew volunteered. "When I started medical school I needed help for some tough subjects. I prayed, and in evening devotions I read, 'If any of you lack wisdom, let him ask of God, that giveth to all men liberally, and upbraideth not; and it shall be given him.' I asked and God honored that promise." He turned to Cindy. "Your turn, honey."

"He passed his exams with honors, too. Hmm, there are so many, which one should I tell you about? I know. It was when Andrew proposed and I needed to make sure he was the man the Lord had chosen for me. I was reading in the book of Job and a phrase jumped out at me: '...the hand of the LORD hath wrought this.' I believed this was the answer and it certainly proved to be God's direction. We've had a good marriage for nearly twelve years."

Lisa quietly slipped out of the room before Colin shared his experience. "I was asked by a businessman to partner with him. I prayed for God's guidance, and the sermon the following Sunday was based on the words, '...This is the way, walk ye in it...' That confirmed my opinion and I accepted the offer. Now I own the company. It was the right decision."

Megan said, "I was always worried that I wouldn't get married. Then I found this promise: 'Delight thyself in the LORD and he shall give thee the desires of thine heart.' I realized that I needed to put the Lord first in my life, and to commit my way to Him and trust Him. Then like it says, He shall 'bring it to pass.' I did. And He did!"

"Those are wonderful, inspiring testimonies," Abby said. "I'm sorry Lisa could not stay. Let's pray for her. I think she's hurting."

The couples left and Peter took advantage of the opportunity to be with Abby. "Let's walk by the sea, Abby. Look, Colin and Megan have the same idea. And here come Andrew and Cindy. What a quiet, relaxing way to finish the day!"

Words were unnecessary as the six of them tramped along the wet sand and breathed deeply. After they turned back, Peter accompanied Abby to her door and took her hand in his. "Thank you for what you are and for all you are doing for us, Abby. I deeply appreciate you. Good night." He gave her hand a gentle squeeze and left.

Abby closed her door and leaned against it. She felt elated with Peter's compliment and the pressure of his hand on hers was sweet to recall. But at the same time she was concerned about his relationship with Lisa. *What were his motives? Time would tell. Wait patiently and see what happens,* she thought as she opened her Bible to read and pray.

Chapter 14

Mt. Carmel

After a continental breakfast of sweet rolls, coffee and fruit in Caesarea, Sam drove the group north along the Mediterranean seacoast. Abby pointed out a Crusader fort where Christians had fought Muslims to keep them from ruling the Holy Land. "If you recall, King Richard the Lionhearted of England figured prominently by fighting bravely in battles against Salahadin, but he was defeated. However, in negotiating for a peaceful settlement, the Muslims opened Jerusalem to the Christians so they could worship at their holy sites.

"At the place where we're going today," she continued, "something special happened on a mountain in the north near the sea. Does anyone remember?"

Megan was watching big waves roll up to the shore and spit spray onto the sand and rocks. Then trees hid the view. She tried to concentrate on Abby's question. "Give us a hint, please," she begged.

"You'll find it on the map in your Bible," Abby answered.

Colin and Andrew pulled out their Bibles. They turned to the back where there were maps of the Holy Land and began to search. Colin knew their approximate location along the coast, so he looked north and ran his finger up to land jutting into the sea. "Here it is. Mt. Carmel."

"You're right. Do you remember what happened there?"

"When Elijah prayed, God sent fire from heaven to

burn up the sacrifice..."

" ...in order to prove He was the living God who answers prayer," Cindy added. "I like the story of that miracle."

Sam turned the van to begin a long, winding climb up the mountain.

"Look at those beautiful scarlet anemones blooming along the roadside," Cindy exclaimed. "Such splendor takes my breath away!"

"Let's stop for a few minutes. It looks like God's flower garden! We can't pick a bouquet because that's a government rule," Abby warned, "but we can enjoy their beauty. I believe I already mentioned that the Christian Arabs say these are the lilies of the field Jesus referred to when He said that Solomon..."

"'...in all his glory was not arrayed like one of these'!" finished Peter with a grin. He remembered that this was one of Abby's favorite verses.

Colin and Andrew took pictures. Then they drove on to the place believed to be where the famous miracle occurred. There was a stone image of Elijah. His arm was stretched upward and in his hand was a sword pointing toward heaven.

Colin thought of the people who had gathered to watch what Elijah was doing. "I like the part where God sends fire and it burns up even the wet wood and stones! Imagine that! What a miracle! How could anyone believe in any other god?"

"Exactly," Peter agreed. "We have God's Word that says if we ask, He will perform miracles for us, too. We know He'll do what is best for us."

"I doubt that," Lisa commented. "There are no miracles taking place today. I asked for one and it never happened."

"Were you certain it was God's will?"

"It was what I wanted, and the Bible says, 'ask, and you will receive.' I asked but I did not receive." Her voice was hard with bitterness.

"I'm sorry, Lisa. If you like, we can pray with you for this miracle."

"It's too late now. Water under the bridge."

A friendly man asked the visitors if they would like to see the conies.

"What are they?" Megan asked.

The man led them to a fence. Beyond it was a pile of rocks on a sloping hill. There, sunning themselves contentedly, were some strange little animals they had never seen before.

"They look like rabbits but they don't have long ears," observed Cindy.

"They hop like rabbits, too," added Andrew as the animals moved about.

"They're mentioned in the Bible, in the book of Psalms. We can look it up when we get back to the van," Abby said.

While they stood there watching, something suddenly frightened the conies. Quickly they dove into hiding places and lay very still. Because they were the same color as the rocks, they were barely visible.

"That's real camouflage," observed Colin. "Do you remember our trip to Sinai? Camels are the same color as the sand and from a distance we could hardly see them. That's called camelflauge!" he chuckled.

Cindy smiled. "It's wonderful that God created the animals with skins that look like the place where they live, to protect them from enemies."

"Exactly," agreed Peter.

Abby thanked the man for showing them the conies and they returned to the van. Megan opened her Bible. "I can't find 'cony' in my concordance," she complained.

"That's because in your translation they may have used a different word. It says in one of the Psalms, ' ...rock-badgers burrow in among the rocks and find protection there.'"

"God certainly takes care of the animals, like He does us," said Megan.

"Right," answered Abby. "Now we're going on to a hotel that has been made into a conference center."

"Well, I hope this one is air-conditioned and has decent food," Lisa remarked.

They drove along a narrow road bordered by tall pine trees and came to a large building. Graceful vines and bright flowers framed the arched porches. A smiling lady came to welcome them and showed them to comfortable rooms.

"My name is Samira. Please let me know if you need anything. Lunch will be served in a few minutes."

Lisa was displeased. "Where is my private bath?"

"None of our rooms here have complete baths, though they all have washbasins. Each floor has bathrooms for men and for women. If you prefer, I can give you a place in one of our new buildings. It is more expensive but it has a private bath and lounge."

"I prefer that. Abby can settle the difference in price. I need space for myself."

"Thank you, Samira," Abby said.

Lunch was buffet style. Everyone made their own sandwiches out of pita bread with roast beef, cheese and condiments. There was potato salad, fruit and cookies, coffee or tea.

After a brief rest, Abby gathered her friends together and suggested they take a brisk walk. "You'll find the nearby Druze village unique."

They passed neat, modern homes. Men with bushy beards and odd turban-like headgear sat in front of souvenir shops.

"These are unusual people," Abby explained. "Their religion is secret. All we know is that it combines Christian and Muslim beliefs. A man in Egypt decided he was the incarnation of God, like Jesus. People believed him and followed his teachings. Today they are called Druze."

Some friendly young girls saw the visitors and

invited them for coffee. Their home was small but comfortably furnished, their mother plump and kindly. Peter explained the gospel simply and they listened with interest. The girls studied English in school and understood easily because he spoke slowly and clearly. They translated for their mother so she would know what he was saying.

The girls were fascinated with Lisa's beautiful blonde hair and one of them reached out to touch it. Lisa recoiled, visibly shuddering. To distract them from the insult, Abby stood quickly and said, "Thank you for your gracious hospitality. Now we must go."

The girls walked to the street with their guests and waved goodbye. Abby led her friends back to the hotel and suggested they relax with a book or games in the lounge.

Samira met them. "We have a conference in progress right now. I think you might enjoy meeting some of the Arab Christians after dinner. They sing and play the piano and accordion and guitar. Their music is lively as well as worshipful."

"Thank you," Abby replied. "We'll be glad to listen in."

After a sumptuous meal of rice and lamb, Lisa declined the invitation to join the crowd and said, "Peter, I need to talk to you."

Abby watched as he followed her to an alcove and sat down beside her. She hoped they would discuss Lisa's need to surrender herself to Christ.

The two couples and Abby followed other guests into the spacious lounge. It was decorated with magnificent Oriental rugs, small wooden tables with inlaid mother-of-pearl, rich wall hangings of colorful designs, shiny brass ornaments and comfortable furniture with lots of pillows.

The Arab Christians who gathered for the songfest recognized Abby and greeted her warmly. She introduced her guests and they were welcomed with the customary kiss on both cheeks and handshake. Everyone was so friendly the couples felt like they had been made a part of the family.

They couldn't understand the words, but some of the tunes sounded familiar so they joined the singing in English. Abby translated one of the hymns for them and the words took on new, special meaning.

> The Words of God make hearts glad,
> Delicious and sweet like a honeycomb.
> Medicine of the bones, it takes away unhappiness,
> Strong medicine for wounds of the heart,
> Words of the doctor for the cripple,
> Comfort of the sorrowful, dispelling poison.
> Robe of goodness and yoke of Christ,
> Rest of the blind, removing anxiety.
>
> Words of the Life-giver, Destroyer of darkness,
> Making all fools wise.
> Guide of the lost and the people.
> Road of heaven, established Truth.
> Words of the rich, rich are the poor.
> Cupboard of gladness and precious treasure,
> Lamp of those who see, and eye of the blind,
> Safe refuge and strong fortress.
>
> Words of kindness, foundation of peace.
> Removing fears, giving security.
> Sign of smiling love to us,
> Nourishment of the soul and water of life.
> Strong words for us in the fight,
> Armor and Shield for us to overcome the devil.
> Heaven and all the mountains may pass away,
> What the great God says is steadfast.

In conclusion, the Arabs sang The Lord's Prayer. The music, in the minor key, was haunting, beautiful and worshipful. When it was finished, everyone remained quiet-- a fitting climax to the evening.

As Abby passed the alcove on her way to her room, she noticed that it was empty. From a window she saw Lisa and Peter walking along a path in the moonlight. *Am I jealous? I don't know. But, oh, what a terrible life he would have if he married her as she is now. Surely he must see that, or is he already blind because yes, from all outward appearances, she is an extremely attractive, beautiful woman. Yet God can change her heart. If this is His plan, I must accept it. Help me, O Lord!*

Chapter 15

Nazareth

The return route from Mt. Carmel to their home base in the valley of Berachah was nearly one hundred miles and consumed most of the morning. Lisa commented that it was the same way they had traveled north.

"You're quite right. But it's the most direct way. We could have cut across and gone east to Galilee, but there are things I want you to see in the central mountains of Samaria. That is on our schedule for tomorrow."

After a light lunch of sandwiches, the friends spent the afternoon relaxing, reading, playing tennis and walking in the adjacent woods. Again, Lisa inveigled Peter into accompanying her along the paths. Her pretended helplessness irritated Abby. She noticed that Peter kindly gave his attention to Lisa, even when she chattered nonsense.

Abby analyzed her thoughts. *I must not let this woman defeat my spiritual walk with Christ. I dare not harbor jealousy. It's a battle I've never fought before and I have to fight it on my knees. O God, help me! Without You I cannot do it, but with You doing it through me, it can be done. Control my thoughts, words and actions. I dwell in You, and You in me. You're the vine, I'm a branch. Pour into me Your love, peace, wisdom, strength, patience and all I need to bear this fruit of the Spirit. With my complete dependence upon You, victory is assured. Thank You, Lord. I rest in Your perfect plan. I commit this situation into Your hands.*

A sense of peace and joy pervaded Abby's heart and she felt the "contentment of commitment."

The next day they were on the road again, heading north.

"Where are we going today?" asked Megan.

"It's a surprise," Abby answered. Her eyes twinkled as she thought of the plans she had made for this day.

"That Arabic music in Mt. Carmel was splendid," Cindy said. "I loved it."

"It kept me awake, and the bed was so hard I tossed and turned all night," Lisa grumbled.

"God spoke to me as I listened to the Lord's Prayer," Colin said. "Forgive as He forgives. I want to remember that in my work."

"Look to your left," Abby said. "The small building on that high hill is called Samuel's Tomb. You all know the story of how God spoke to him when he was a young boy."

"How does God speak to us?" asked Lisa.

"When we read the Bible or when we pray," answered Peter. "Sometimes He uses things that happen to us to show us what He wants us to know or to do."

"How could He be so cruel? What has happened to me shouldn't happen to anyone. My circumstances have taught me that you can't trust anyone, even God."

"You can't mean that, Lisa. In time, you will understand why God has permitted this disappointment and heartache in your life. It is your responsibility to ask Him to help you learn the spiritual lesson He wants to teach you."

"Well, it's a tough way to learn, I assure you."

"Yes. We understand. And we are praying for you."

"Thank you, but don't bother. It won't do any good," she retorted with stinging sarcasm.

The road wound up and down, around curves and over the mountains. Lisa was carsick again and they waited patiently while she lost her breakfast. "Ugh, I hate this. Why can't Sam drive more slowly? He deliberately speeds to make me feel wretched."

"No, he doesn't, Lisa. Carsickness can happen to anyone. We understand and we're not blaming anyone. Just try to make the best of it." Andrew's words of attempted consolation fell on deaf ears.

"This lush valley of cultivated fields we're driving through is called Lebonah, or the Valley of the Dancers," Abby explained.

"I don't remember that in the Bible. What happened? Tell us the story, please," Megan urged.

"Jacob had twelve sons, as you know. Each one became the head of his family, or tribe. After many years the tribe of Benjamin grew wicked. The other tribes fought with them and only six hundred Benjamites were left. They hid in a cave for several months until the other tribes decided it was time to let them marry and have families. They found four hundred young women for the weddings, but two hundred were left without wives."

"Peter, would you like to continue?" Abby asked.

"Right. The Israelites made a plan. Every year there was a feast in Shiloh where the tabernacle was located. They told the two hundred men to hide in the vineyards. When young girls came to the valley to celebrate the feast and to dance, each man was to catch a girl for himself and take her home to be his bride. And that's exactly what they did!"

"How romantic!" Cindy exclaimed. "I like that story."

The road led through the mountains of Samaria. Sam carefully took the curves slowly so there could be no complaints from the front seat passenger.

"We're entering Nablus now, an old city that used to be called Shechem. Here's a church we want to visit."

They climbed down steep steps to a large room. Beside an old well and bucket stood a pretty young woman wearing Palestinian clothes. Her dress was a deep blue with cross-stitch embroidery in varied colors covering the bodice and wide panels of the skirt. A long white veil covered her hair but did not hide her face. She offered to pull up water for them to taste.

Abby said, "This is the place where Jesus sat and talked with the Samaritan woman."

Megan was thrilled to have a drink from that same well. So was Cindy. Lisa refused, mumbling disapproval of germ-laden implements and possible amoeba in the water.

"Jesus knew everything the Samaritan woman had done. He knows everything we do, too," Abby commented.

"How can He know everything? I don't want Him to know some of the things I've done," Lisa admitted.

Peter answered, "God sees and knows everything. Yet His everlasting love and forgiveness are overwhelming."

"Overwhelming, all right," Colin agreed.

Lisa was quiet, pondering these thought-provoking concepts.

"Nablus is famous for its treats the Arabs serve on special occasions, like birthdays, holidays, engagement parties and weddings. Sam is taking us to a shop for some baklava." Abby passed around wedges of the sticky, crunchy sweet. "It's made with thin flaky sheets of what used to be called Swedish pastry, now said to be 'puff' by some people. It's baked between layers of nuts and cinnamon and then soaked with syrup." Everyone praised it.

Everyone except Lisa, of course. By now the rest knew she'd criticize, regardless of how good something might be. She ran true to form. "This is far too sweet, and bad for your teeth, let alone your health." She promptly threw her piece out the window as they drove away.

"To our left is the Samaritan community. Originally an Assyrian king captured the Israelites living in Samaria and replaced them with Babylonians. They were enemies of the Jews. You can understand why it was surprising that Jesus would talk to the Samaritan woman at the well. The people are distinguished by their long hair and beard. They accept only the Torah, or Pentateuch--the five books of Moses. At one time they had a temple on Mt. Gerizim and they still observe the Passover there. They dig a trench and before they slaughter seven sheep the priest reads from the book of Exodus.

"Opposite us is Mt. Ebal. Moses commanded the people to offer a blessing on Mt. Gerazim and a curse on Mt. Ebal. Later, Joshua built an altar on Mt. Ebal, offered sacrifices and wrote a copy of the law on the stones."

Water dripped from huge boulders close to the road. Miniature iris had popped up here and there. Masses of tiny little yellow and purple wildflowers carpeted fields and olive groves.

They stopped beside an old well near Dothan and Peter read the story of Joseph and his brothers.

"Why did God let that happen to Joseph?"

"Lisa, God had a reason. He was preparing Joseph to save his family. He blessed him in the end. He always does that."

"No, He doesn't," she replied emphatically with sarcasm.

"Look at those sheep resting beside a stream, just like in Psalm 23," observed Andrew.

"And they're lying down in thick green grass," added Cindy.

Sam stopped, and the men took pictures. A Bedouin shepherd was nearby. Abby greeted the man just as a young boy came riding up on his donkey. He spoke to the shepherd and then invited them to come to his home. They gladly accepted in spite of Lisa's objections, and picked their way through a stony field to a big tent. A young woman came to welcome them. She seated them on striped rugs in front of the fire.

"My name is Usif. It means Joseph in your language," the boy explained. "This is my mother. You met my father. He was with the sheep."

"We're happy to meet you. These are my friends," Abby said.

Joseph's father came from the field and sent an older son to tend the animals. He invited the guests for food. Abby politely refused, but he insisted, so she accepted. Lisa stared at her, her eyes narrowed slits of disapproval. "I cannot endure this," she whispered, and walked out of the tent to wait in the van.

"I'm sorry," Abby apologized. "Please forgive the lady. She does not feel well."

Megan watched Joseph's mother put eggs into the hot ashes of the fire. She mixed water with wheat flour and a pinch of salt, patted a ball of it paper-thin and slapped it onto a metal lid like an inverted wok, to bake over the fire.

A little duck waged a pecking war with a chick and then ran to hide behind several boxes. A small child tumbled about with a lively newborn kid.

Abby pulled out her Wordless Book and explained the colors. Joseph's Mother's eyes lit up when she saw the white page representing a clean heart. She pointed to her white veil and said, "Yes, we must have a clean heart like this in order to go to heaven to live with God." She had responded with understanding and Abby's heart gave a joyful bound.

Suddenly there was a loud explosion and ashes from the fire flew all over Megan and Cindy. They jumped and shouted, "What happened?"

"Don't worry," laughed Joseph, "it was only the eggs exploding. They're ready to eat now." He gave the guests each one. They were hard to peel and tasted a bit tough. His mother brought several big round breads, a bowl of yogurt and a bowl of butter.

"We use the products of our livestock: eggs, milk, meat and wool," he explained. "We tear off a small piece of bread, dip it in one of the bowls and eat the whole piece. It would not be proper to bite off part of the piece and dip it in again, because we all use the same bowl."

Nazareth

How good the food tasted! While they were eating, a donkey began to bray. Megan giggled and they all laughed at the shrill, raspy noise.

"It sounds like a rusty gate," chuckled Andrew. "What's the donkey's name?"

"Elmer."

"Elmer? Where did you get that name?"

"We sit in grandfather's tent over there and watch TV in the evenings. We don't have electricity so we use a generator. I heard the name 'Elmer' on a program the day my little donkey was born."

They thanked their new friends for the delicious food and Abby gave them an Arabic Bible, along with a small Wordless Book for Joseph. "Now you can remember the story I explained," she said.

"That was another highlight of our trip," Colin remarked as they drove away.

"You can say that again!" Lisa added. "I feel like I'm a black sheep, the way I'm ignored."

"Too bad. Join us next time, then," Colin answered.

"You'll like our next stop," promised Abby as they passed miles of plowed fields and began curving up and around a steep mountain. "Guess who lived here and probably played as a child in these hills?"

"Jesus?" ventured Cindy.

"Right. How did you know?"

"Just a wild guess."

"Then this is Nazareth!" figured Andrew.

"Right again. We're in Galilee."

Sam guided the van to a parking place. "Let's walk through the market to the churches where there are special things to remind us of Jesus' boyhood," Abby suggested.

They looked through a glass and saw what was said to be a replica of Joseph's carpenter shop. On a lower floor was a room like the one where Jesus might have lived. The walls of a big church exhibited elaborate paintings donated by many countries of the world.

Comforting Arms

In a small restaurant they lunched on kabobs of lamb, potatoes and onions. Shops along the sidewalks displayed souvenirs: brass plates and vases, pictures of the churches, postcards and jewelry.

"What next?" asked Megan as they returned to the van.

"Another surprise," Abby answered. They wound down the back of the mountain and passed a few villages, then stopped in a narrow cobblestone street beside a church.

Inside were huge stone jars. "Can you figure out what these might be and where we are?" Abby asked. "I'll give you a hint. Jesus and His family were invited to a wedding here."

"Of course, it's Cana and…" Peter began.

"…and the jars were full of water that Jesus turned into wine," finished Colin. "Sorry. I didn't mean to interrupt."

"Exactly. Probably not these jars, but some like them," Abby said. Arabs still use them for storing supplies. This was Jesus' first recorded miracle. Now let's go on to where we'll spend the night."

The main road led past a Syrian tank captured by Israelis during the previous war, large olive groves, fields and fisheries. Sky-blue water appeared in the distance as they curved down into the city of Tiberius.

"We're by the sea where Jesus performed many miracles."

"Ah, the Sea of Galilee," Peter said.

"Can we swim in it?" asked Megan.

"Tomorrow," Abby replied. "We'll have a leisurely day exploring and remembering all the exciting things that took place here. There's our hotel. I'll meet you all for dinner, then we can have devotions in one of the lounges."

Chapter 16

Galilee

The next morning Sam drove the friends around the Sea of Galilee. Beyond the hotels, flowering bushes and trees bordered the shoreline. They passed a little domed building half-buried in the dirt. Cindy read the sign, "Home of Mary Magdala."

"Is this really where she lived?" asked Megan. "Jesus cast out seven demons from that Mary Magdalene?"

"Yes, it could have been her little home, the place where she lived. He performed several other miracles in this area, too."

They stopped at Tabgha. A huge grindstone was on display in the yard. "That must be like the one Samson had to turn after the Philistines captured him and made him blind," Colin said.

"But it looks terribly heavy. How could he have pulled it around in a circle?" asked Megan.

"Especially when his strength was gone," Cindy added.

"As his hair grew long again, his strength probably returned," Peter suggested.

They entered the church. A floor mosaic pictured a fish and bread. "Oh, this must be where Jesus fed the five thousand!" Megan guessed.

"Yes. The inscription reads,
> 'Jesus, Love incredible, is constrained
> To help wherever He sees
> His children to be in want.

> But He waits for empty hearts,
> For hands stretched out,
> Wherein He may lay His gifts.'"

"That's so meaningful it brings tears to my eyes," said Cindy.

"Then you'll appreciate the next one at St. Peter's church," Abby said. They stood quietly for a few moments, then returned to the van and continued driving around the lake. "We're coming to the church now. Jesus built a fire on the shore and cooked breakfast for His disciples while they were fishing. The inscription above the door reads:

> 'The waves are whispering of the hour,
> The greatest that will ever be.
> The Lord, He cometh down again.
> He sees the fields to harvest, white,
> The trees, the flowers in beauty light.
> The waves are calling louder.
> They call: The promise is fulfilled!
> O come, Lord Jesus, come!'"

"I like the part about the promise being fulfilled. God always does that, like we've said before. He keeps His Word!" Peter remarked.

"We don't have to drive far to find the hill where Jesus taught the Beatitudes to a crowd of people. Let's sit down on this lush grass overlooking the sea. Why don't we all read together the Sermon on the Mount."

'Blessed are the poor in spirit: for theirs is the kingdom of heaven.

Blessed are they that mourn: for they shall be comforted.

Blessed are the meek: for they shall inherit the earth.

Blessed are they which do hunger and thirst after righteousness: for they shall be filled.

Blessed are the merciful: for they shall obtain mercy.

Blessed are the pure in heart: for they shall see God.

Blessed are the peacemakers: for they shall be called the children of God.

Blessed are they which are persecuted for righteousness' sake: for theirs is the kingdom of God.

Blessed are ye, when men shall revile you, and persecute you, and shall say all manner of evil against you falsely, for my sake.

Rejoice, and be exceeding glad: for great is your reward in heaven: for so persecuted they the prophets which were before you.'

"Which of these verses is your favorite?" Abby asked.

"I like the 'pure in heart' one," Megan answered. "I pray every day for Jesus to help me keep my heart clean."

"I choose 'merciful,'" said Andrew. "Using medical skills, I have an opportunity to tell people about Jesus, because He's the One Who is loving and kind and comforts us when we hurt."

Colin was thoughtful. "I have to be a peacemaker where I work, because my employees sometimes need an arbitrator. It's my responsibility to tell them about the One who can provide peace in their heart."

"I 'hunger and thirst after righteousness,' and it seems like I'm never satisfied," Cindy admitted. "I always want more!"

"But that's good," Peter commended. "We all need daily spiritual food. Your hunger and thirst are justified. This is how you grow in the Christian life."

Lisa was hesitant. At last she admitted, "I'm 'poor in spirit,' and I'm not proud of it. My spiritual life is nil even though I claim to be a Christian. I go to church and give my tithe and I always thought that was enough. But on this trip I've been learning that you all have a personal relationship with Christ that I don't have. And I know I need it."

"It's yours for the asking, Lisa," Peter said. "Would you like to pray right now?"

"No. I want to think about what it might mean. I'm not ready yet."

Abby turned to Peter. "And your special one?"

"My students always kept me from being proud with their questions and ability to see through a person. So 'meekness,' which means humility, is what I pray for. When we harbor pride, God has a way of humbling us. I've learned this the hard way."

"Being a widow has taught me to depend upon the Lord for comfort. Loneliness causes me to 'mourn' occasionally, but I turn to God's Word for strength and help." Abby stood up. "Now on to Capernaum. A Bible character you know about lived there and you'll see where his home used to be."

They rode a short distance and then walked down a path among ancient ruins. Abby gave them a clue. "This disciple loved Jesus but at the trial he was afraid, and denied he even knew Him."

"It was Peter," Cindy said.

"Yes. And here are the possible remains of his home. Remember how Jesus healed Peter's mother-in-law of a fever? She immediately got up and helped make food for the disciples."

Abby pointed to more ruins where a few pillars and arches stood. "Jesus preached in a synagogue like the one that used to be over there."

Peter panned a video of the two couples perched on one of the ancient walls. They drove along the lake to a wooded picnic area. At a nearby lunch stand they ordered roast beef sandwiches and soft drinks. While they ate, Abby suggested that they try to think of more miracles Jesus had performed in the vicinity.

"He quieted the storm when the disciples thought they were drowning. He said, 'Peace, be still' and the wind and waves obeyed Him."

"Right, Megan. What's another one?"

Galilee

"The disciples had fished all night and caught nothing. Then Jesus told them to put down their nets and they caught so many fish the nets began to break."

"Good, Andrew. Any more?"

Peter added, "Peter wanted to walk on the water when he saw Jesus doing it. But he looked down instead of at Jesus and he began to sink. That's a good lesson to remember. If we look at our problems we sink in discouragement, but if we look to Jesus He will help us."

"Along these shores Jesus healed the nobleman's son and the Roman soldier's servant," added Abby as she watched men in the distance mending their nets and preparing small boats for fishing. The lake was bordered by a shoreline of rocks, trees and oleander bushes interspersed with a diversity of fishing boats, hotels, kibbutzim, banana and date palm groves.

"Now how about a swim before we leave? The lake looks calm and inviting."

Back in Tiberius they browsed among the shops and then returned to their hotel. "It's nearly dinnertime," Abby said. "After you've freshened up, we'll meet in the lounge and then go to eat 'Peter's Fish' at a nearby restaurant. The tables are outside, right beside the sea."

"Well, Peter, are remarks in order about this fish being named after you?" laughed Colin as they began the meal.

"Hardly," he grinned. "But this meal is 'on me.' Enjoy. I've settled it with Abby."

While they were savoring the treat, some young men rowed their boat close beside the low seawall and stopped. A few fish lay in the bow of the boat. With one long look at lovely Lisa, the men invited her to go out on the lake with them. She half rose from the table but Abby quickly declined for her, with thanks. After they pulled away, she promised they would all take a boat trip the next day.

"And why can't you let me decide for myself whether or not I want to do something?" Lisa stormed.

Comforting Arms

"Because I'm responsible for your safety. You could have been raped or murdered, to put it bluntly."

"Oh." A subdued Lisa remained at a loss for further comments, much to the surprised relief of the whole team.

Abby kept her promise. The next morning they climbed aboard a large ferryboat along with many other passengers. Soon they were well out into the middle of the six-mile-wide lake.

"Just think, Cindy, we're sailing on the Sea of Galilee like Jesus and His disciples did!" Megan said contentedly as they leaned against the rail and gazed into the water.

"Yes, but this is a bigger boat and they didn't have an engine to provide their power."

Suddenly the wind began to blow and the waves turned choppy. The boat rocked up and down violently, nearly jerking people off their feet. Benches on the deck were fastened down or they would have started sliding. Frightened people scattered and ran to find shelter from the rain. The waves rose higher and an angry wind tossed the boat furiously.

Cindy staggered along the slick deck to find Andrew. Megan stood petrified and clung tightly to the rail until Colin came to rescue her. He put his arms around her and slowly edged her to a seat. Her voice shook as she said, "This must be like it was when Jesus made the storm stop!" She was trembling. "Now I know how the disciples must have felt! We aren't going to sink, are we?"

"My dear, don't be afraid. Isn't that what Jesus said? You know He's the same today as He was then. He'll take care of us."

Colin's assurance was comforting, and his protecting arm gave his wife confidence as she watched the awesome storm. But as quickly as it had begun, it also quickly began to blow itself away. The rough waves calmed down and the ship no longer lurched about. Megan began to relax but she still held Colin's hand tightly. She was glad when they reached land safely.

Colin remarked, "I'm convinced God gave us a taste of what it was really like in Bible times. What a sensational adventure!"

"Where were you during that awful storm?" Megan asked Cindy.

"Inside with Andrew. I thought we'd both go down together!"

"And you, Lisa?"

"I was terrified! I ran to Peter and he found a seat for us and sat beside me. I could not have endured that violent storm alone. It was a horrible experience, not knowing if we'd live or die."

"And what about you, Abby?" asked Peter.

"I waited in a corner and prayed for the Lord to have mercy. I can't swim and I've never enjoyed being on the water. I have to trust God for His help at a time like this."

Peter wished he had looked after Abby and stayed with her. *It must have been an ordeal for her. She's a brave woman. I take my hat off to her. This tour has been a difficult one for her, having to endure all of Lisa's cutting remarks. She has held up remarkably and shown a Christ-like attitude. What a shining testimony of forgiveness and loving kindness she is! I think I'm falling in love with her. Is this Your will for me, Lord? If it is, please confirm it. And cause her to feel the same way.*

Sam had the van ready when they disembarked. Before they began the long drive toward Jerusalem and on to the guest home, they stopped at a place where the sea flowed into the Jordan River. A baptismal service was taking place. They watched white-robed people hold onto chains for safety against the strong current as they waded out into the water. It was impressive to hear them tell how Jesus had changed them and they wanted to let the world know that they were now His followers.

People gathered around and sat on tiered stone steps to watch and sing songs in their own language. The Arab Christians finished their service by singing, "I Have Decided to Follow Jesus," and Abby explained to her friends that the chorus had significant meaning for Arab and Jewish believers because of the threat of opposition and persecution by parents, friends, even co-workers.

"It takes extreme courage to make that final step and sever familiar ties. It could mean a loss of friends, a job, home and family. Relatives stole a Muslim believer's passport so he could not leave the country. Whenever he went outside he continually looked around to see if he was being followed. He was in constant fear of bodily harm, even death. His wife was kidnapped and threatened. Later when she visited her family, they locked her in the house so she could not return to her husband."

"I had no idea such things happened. It's shocking," Cindy said. "We are free to make our own decisions. What a contrast between Christianity and other religions."

African Christians arrived in a bus. They were dressed in colorful robes and began chanting lively tunes of joy and praise as they prepared for their baptismal service.

"Can't we stay longer?" Cindy asked. "This is fascinating. I love it."

"I wish we could, but we've a long drive ahead as soon as we finish lunch," Abby answered.

The road led along the border between Israel, the river and Jordan on the other side.

"What is all that barbed wire for?" asked Megan.

"It deters people who try to cross from Jordan to Israel. Do you see the wide space between the two fences? I think mines are planted in the ground to keep terrorists from trying to get through."

A jeep-load of soldiers patrolled the fence. Their vehicle was dragging a strange contraption.

"What are they doing?" Megan asked.

"They're scraping the ground. If anyone does climb the fence to get across, his footprints will show in the dust. They guard the border carefully. See the sandbags on the roof of that house? It's probably an army post."

"Look, Megan, caves in the mountains. You'd like to investigate them, wouldn't you?" Colin grinned and waved to friendly farmers working in their fields.

It was almost dark when they reached the guest home. Again Peter thanked Abby for more unique stories to add to his treasure-chest of memories.

After a late dinner and devotions, Lisa cornered Peter. Abby saw them leave the lounge together. In her room she knelt beside her bed and prayed for God's help. *I admit I admire and respect him very much. I can only pray that You, Lord, will handle this situation, because I cannot.* In answer, she seemed to hear Him say, "*Then let me.*"

Chapter 17

Gaza

Abby said, "Today our first stop is the valley of Elah. I'm sure you all know what happened here. Two armies were camped on these hills, ready for battle. The Israelites probably were to our left, the Philistines over there on the right. David killed Goliath and the Philistines were defeated."

"What a simple yet meaningful story. We may have giants in our life, such as physical, emotional, financial or spiritual problems. But God has a unique way of enabling us to overcome and defeat them joyfully when we trust Him," Peter said.

Lisa frowned. "I cannot exhibit joy because God has not solved my problems. I've tried but gotten nowhere. I need your help, Peter."

"You need to trust Him to help you, Lisa."

"Yes, I guess you're right. I haven't done that. Please show me how."

At last perhaps she's beginning to understand, Abby thought. *Maybe our patience and prayers are having an effect.*

Peter replied, "I'll do all I possibly can, but you are the one who must commit yourself to Christ and let Him control your life and every decision you make."

"I'm sure you're right. Someday I'll do that. Not yet. There is something I want first and I intend to have it. Believe me, I deserve some happiness."

Abby silently groaned. *So she understands, but still she's not ready to make a commitment, because her selfish desires are hindering spiritual progress.*

Abby pointed out a large orchard of plum trees in the opposite valley. "Their branches were loaded with masses of pink blossoms when I was here earlier last year. The fruit should be ripe in another month or six weeks. They are what the Arabs call 'Santa Rosa,' deep purplish-red on the outside, pinkish-red on the inside and simply the most delicious, juicy plums in the world!"

They wandered into a field below the hill where David probably found his brothers camped with Saul's army. It was filled with exquisite wildflowers, thyme and dill plants. Cindy found masses of rare purple lupines. She had to suppress the urge to pick a bouquet.

Suddenly a frightened partridge flew up in front of Lisa and she screamed. Automatically, she rushed to Peter, throwing herself at him, fiercely thrusting her arms around his shoulders and burying her head on his chest. Her expensive perfume made him aware of her closeness and he tried to loosen her tight hold.

When the others saw what had frightened her, they gazed in awe at the bird's beauty.

"Look, Lisa, it's only a wild partridge," Peter assured her, and he gently unwound her clinging arms so he could step away. This woman is deliberately tempting me, he thought. *O God, be my help and provide the strength I need to deal with her as a Christian man should. She depends upon me for support. Give me Your holy wisdom to say and do the things You would have me to. I do not want to hurt or offend her, but I'm getting desperate enough to do something drastic to curtail her flirtations and brazen actions.*

"Here's its nest," Colin announced as he found the place where the bird had been sitting, "and there are eggs in it!"

"Naturally we won't disturb them," Abby said firmly. "Let's go away so the mother can come back and keep those developing chicks warm."

Back at the narrow bridge where the van was parked, Abby led them down the bank. "From this stream David picked up those five smooth stones he put in his bag to use for killing Goliath."

"I'm going to pick up five stones to use as an illustration for a message I've been thinking about. It's on 'Giants in our Lives,'" Peter said as he put them into his pocket. "Now I'll have to find a slingshot."

"You and Colin both want one. We'll be going to Bethany in a couple of days and I'll show you a shop where they are sold," Abby said.

The road led on to Zorah, Samson's birthplace. "It's called Sorek now," Abby explained as they stopped beside a cave so camouflaged in the hill it was hardly noticeable. They entered and found it was a huge lengthy cavern full of stalactites and stalagmites in various stages of development.

"You probably know their odd shapes are formed by minerals in the water dripping from the ceiling." Abby pointed out imaginary images. "Can you visualize Bible characters these figures might resemble? Over there might be Moses holding the Ten Commandments, and here is young David, then Elijah with his sword."

"What a fascinating display," Megan said.

"How simple can you get?" Lisa smirked, her lips thin with annoyance.

On their way again they passed giant sand dunes, their tops scalloped and sides rippled by the wind. Farther along were Bedouin tents, a camel train and another lady like one they had seen wearing a veil of coins sewn onto cloth strips that streamed down in front of her face.

Then came a sudden glimpse of the Mediterranean Sea. For several miles there were occasional views of the waves dancing in the sunlight. More sand dunes appeared.

Gaza

"Gaza welcomes you," Andrew read on a sign. "Well, we know Samson came here. We saw where he lived and this is where he died."

"You're right. The Philistines captured him when Delilah gave the signal. She had cut his hair and caused him to lose his great strength."

"He should not have disobeyed God and told her his secret," Megan said.

"Yes, especially one God gave him to protect," Peter added. "After Samson suffered in prison he must have asked God to forgive him because we know what happened in the end."

"His hair grew long again. Maybe the Philistines didn't understand that was where God stored his strength. Consequently, he pulled down the pillars of the temple and destroyed more people when he died than he had during his whole lifetime." Megan drew a deep breath of satisfaction as she finished the story.

Sam drove out of the town and stopped along a clean sandy beach bordered by palm trees.

"Can we swim here?" asked Cindy. "We've learned to always bring along our swimsuits."

"I'm afraid not. We can wade and hunt for shells. But because of the strong undertow it's not safe to go into the water. People who have disregarded that advice have been swept out to sea and drowned. Last year two young men lost their lives that way. But we can take off our shoes and go barefoot on the sand. There are heaps of shells washed up by the strong waves. Some of them have tiny holes and they could be strung on a ribbon to wear around your neck or be put on a key chain," suggested Abby.

"That's a good idea. I'll collect some to give to my friends," Megan said. Cindy agreed and began picking up lovely colored shells in shades of pink, rust, pale blue, cream and brown. The men rolled up their pant legs and knelt to build a sandcastle.

Comforting Arms

"How childish can you get?" Lisa sighed with disgust and walked away by herself. She sat on a rock, her expression one of disdainful condescension and boredom.

The town of Gaza was unique. They walked through the markets where food and merchandise were for sale. Ladies carrying supplies in bags and buckets on their head were intent on haggling for their purchases. Handmade rugs were displayed outside shops where they were being produced.

The fragrant odor of kabobs roasting over charcoal smelled tempting. Abby bought enough for everyone enjoy. Except Lisa. She refused to touch the tasty chunks of lamb, potatoes and onions. Abby had anticipated that reaction and offered her a sandwich.

"I made it for you this morning before we left," she said. Even that gesture of kindness was unappreciated and thanks were left unsaid.

Late in the afternoon, they headed toward the guest home. Sam stopped in a remote area and Megan wondered what was coming next. Abby guided them along a narrow path to a huge limestone cave. It led to a series of smaller caves. Some of the ceilings looked like they had been carved with sharp instruments. Faded printing decorated a few of the walls.

"What have we here?" asked Peter.

"Early Christians may have hidden in these caves from fanatics who wanted to torture and kill them," Abby explained.

"Because they followed Jesus," Cindy assumed.

"Yes. We know from stories in the Bible how Saul hunted down Christians and took them in chains to the high priests in Jerusalem to be punished and thrown into prison.

"From what we read in the book of Hebrews, some of the Old Testament characters were also heroes of the faith, because they suffered and were persecuted when they obeyed God. Let's sit down on these rocks and listen to what the

Bible says." Abby pulled out her little New Testament and asked Peter to read.

"'And what more shall I say? I do not have time to tell about Gideon, Barak, Samson, Jephtha, David, Samuel and the prophets, who through faith conquered kingdoms, administered justice, and gained what was promised; who shut the mouths of lions, quenched the fury of the flames and escaped the edge of the sword; whose weakness was turned to strength; and who became powerful in battle and routed foreign armies. Women received back their dead, raised to life again. Others were tortured and refused to be released, so that they might gain a better resurrection.

"'Some faced jeers and flogging, while still others were chained and put in prison. They were stoned; they were sawed in two; they were put to death by the sword. They went about in sheepskins and goatskins, destitute, persecuted and mistreated--the world was not worthy of them. They wandered in deserts and mountains; and in caves and holes in the ground. These were all commended for their faith...'"

"Whew! They did that because they loved God!" Colin commented.

"Yes," Peter said. "They believed and obeyed God regardless of threats or persecution or even death. They were martyrs. Down through the ages there have been more brave heroes and heroines than we can count. Probably many we do not know about. Even today in some fanatical countries of the world Christians are being persecuted, imprisoned, tortured and killed for their faith!"

"We'll meet them when we get to heaven!" Cindy smiled in anticipation.

"We certainly will. Won't we have a great time hearing all they have to tell us! That will be better than reading about it or even seeing where it happened."

The sun was low in the west as they turned toward Bethlehem. They drove through a valley where hundreds of doves perched on the telephone wires. "Let's call this the Valley of the Doves," suggested Megan.

Comforting Arms

"That's a good name for it," Abby agreed. "You know doves represent the Holy Spirit in the Bible."

"Yes," Peter said. "When John baptized Jesus, God sent a dove representing the Holy Spirit to rest upon Him. Poor people brought doves for a sacrificial offering in the temple. That represented reconciliation to God. A dove is also the symbol of peace and of tender and devoted affection. You've seen it pictured on valentines?"

"Oh yes! Colin gave me a beautiful one last year," Megan exclaimed with bubbling enthusiasm. She leaned over and kissed her husband soundly.

"Please, spare us," Lisa groaned as she stared at the stony mountains they were driving through. "I suppose those rocks represent people's hard hearts?"

"Don't torture yourself," Abby said sympathetically. "God can melt even the hardest heart. We're going to have a good dinner tonight to top off the day. I think Julia said it would be 'upside-down.'"

"Upside-down? What in the world would that be?" asked Megan.

"A surprise," Abby answered. "It's one of my favorite Arab dishes. I think you'll like it, too. It makes my mouth water just to think about how tasty it will be!"

"Well, I hope it's cooked properly for the rest of you. Personally, I simply cannot tolerate this Eastern food. It tastes like garbage. She'll have to make something else for me to eat. I cannot go hungry."

Abby did not reply. There was no pleasing the woman.

The meal was a huge success. Lamb, rice and cauliflower were layered and cooked in a big round, deep pan. When it was ready, it was turned upside-down onto a platter, where it stayed in the shape of a cake. The guests were delighted. But true to form, Lisa complained about her leftover chicken dinner.

"Was this refrigerated? It might be tainted. I'm not sure I can eat it."

"Don't worry, Lisa, it's been carefully preserved and it's not contaminated," Julia assured her.

Lisa stole away as soon as she had eaten, and stayed in her room until after devotions. Then she appeared and Abby saw her motioning to Peter. They sauntered outside to a bench beneath the trees.

For the third time, Abby fell to her knees in her room. Searching her heart, she knew she felt a deep, growing love for Peter. *Oh Lord,* she prayed silently with tears dripping onto the bedspread, *help me to exhibit loving patience and sympathetic understanding for both Peter and Lisa. This is the hardest test You've ever given me. I want to be brave and strong. You are the source of all wisdom and strength. I'm determined to draw from your rich supply everything I need to accept courageously whatever the outcome may be. May I be assured of Your perfect will in this matter? That is all I ask.*

Unable to sleep, Abby quietly went down the back stairs and found a seat on an old log in the woods. She was unaware of Peter's approach until he was beside her.

"I saw you leave and I wanted to talk with you. May I join you?"

"But you and Lisa? Where is she?"

"Lisa has gone inside. I've tried to counsel her by pointing out from the Scriptures what she needs to do and how God can solve her problems. She adamantly refuses to make a definite commitment to Christ. I'm doing the best I can for her. I hope you understand that."

"Yes, Peter, I do understand. May God give you the wisdom you need. Thank you for sharing that with me."

"Would you mind telling me about yourself? Where were you born? I'm interested in your background," Peter said.

"I'm a Buckeye!" Abby laughed.

"I've no idea what that means."

"Anyone born in Ohio is called that, because Ohio is known as the Buckeye State. There were lots of buckeye trees in the early days when settlers first penetrated that area. In fact, at Christmas we make candy called buckeyes. It's peanut butter, powdered sugar and butter rolled into a one-inch ball and coated with melted chocolate except for a round area at the top. It looks like a buckeye."

"It sounds delicious."

"It is!"

"Your parents were Christians?"

"Yes. I accepted Jesus as my Savior when I was eleven years old. The rest of my story you've already heard from our discussions. How about your early life?"

"It was much the same as yours. I was born in South Wales. My parents were dedicated Christians and when I was very young they taught me to love Jesus. I always wanted to teach. God put in my heart a special love for training young men for the ministry and that is where He has placed me."

"Nothing could be more rewarding, I'm sure."

"God gives each one of His children a special gift and if we're willing, He utilizes that talent."

"You're quite right. Knowing we're doing what He wants us to do gives us deep joy and peace. I call it 'the contentment of commitment.'"

"Precisely."

Abby knew it was late but she didn't want the conversation to end. God had given her this opportunity to share with Peter and she felt it strengthened the bond between them. She hoped the feeling was mutual. As she stood up, Peter held out his hand and clasped hers. They walked hand in hand back to the lounge and he looked deeply into her eyes as he said goodnight.

Chapter 18

Jericho

A steep road curved east down the Judean mountains. Modern buildings and tiny shops gave way to hills dotted with sheep and goats nibbling bits of grass.

"Over there's a Bedouin tent! I'm glad we got to visit one--no, two," said Cindy.

"Where are we going? Look! There's a sign. It says, 'sea level.' So we're under the sea now! That's what our Joe would say," giggled Megan as the van continued to wind downward.

"You're right," Abby answered, "we're going below what would be the level of the Mediterranean Sea, which is about forty-five miles west."

"Little Gina would ask, 'Why doesn't the sea overrun the land and fill up this low part of the earth?'" Megan said.

Peter chuckled. "A logical question. You probably told them that God has set boundaries for the seas and the water must remain within them."

"Indeed. Look, there's a lake!"

"It's the Dead Sea," Abby smiled. "We've come about eighteen miles from Jerusalem."

"I've heard about it but I don't remember the details," Megan said.

"The Jordan river flows into it but there is no outlet, no river nor ocean for it to flow into. The extremely hot sun evaporates the water so quickly that it leaves a lot of salt and mineral deposits. Nothing can live in it."

"And that's why it's called the Dead Sea, my dear," Colin added.

"Can we go right up to it and see some salt?" asked Cindy.

"Yes, we will. But right now we're on our way to a place where one of the miracles in the Bible happened. This was a different kind of miracle. You'll soon guess what it was."

Sam turned down a long road past barren land. A few scrawny bushes and spindly acacia trees survived here and there.

"The sign says, 'Jericho,'" read Andrew.

"So the miracle you mentioned must be connected with Zaccheus?" Peter looked at Abby.

"You're right. This is where he lived. And there is a big sycamore tree like the kind Zaccheus may have climbed. The miracle I'm thinking of is how Jesus knew him by name and how He changed his heart."

"It's comforting that He knows my name, like He knew all about the woman at the well in Samaria," Megan said.

"Yes, and He changes our hearts. He changed mine," Colin added.

Lisa curled her lips disdainfully. "That's impossible, I think."

"With God all things are possible," countered Peter.

"If you say so. But I'm not convinced. I still say He cannot change mine."

They passed a tree covered with cascading sprays of bright purple flowers. "That's bougainvillea," Abby said.

In the center of town merchants displayed tempting varieties of fruit arranged in neat rows. "Jericho is famous for its fresh fruit and vegetables," Abby said as she bought some big, delicious-looking oranges from a little shop.

Sam parked outside the town and they climbed up a short bare hill. In a deep excavated fissure, the ruins of eight

Jericho

ancient cities of Jericho were squeezed into layers, each on top of the other.

"Joshua and the soldiers of Israel marched around for six days quietly and then on the seventh..."

"They marched around seven times and shouted and God made the walls fall down flat!" finished Megan. "Is this really where it happened?"

"Yes. And what is so amazing is that the wall was about six feet thick and thirty feet high. Seemingly impregnable. Yet God made it collapse."

"See that mountain over there?" Abby pointed to a high one beyond them. "That's called the Mount of Temptation."

"The devil took Jesus there to see if He would bow down and worship him. But Jesus refused," Andrew added.

"Why would Jesus have to be tempted?" asked Lisa.

Abby turned to Peter. "Would you like to answer that?"

"I believe God permitted that for our benefit. Jesus suffered temptation so that He would be able to help those who are tempted. He gives us courage to resist doing what we know is wrong."

"But that's the hard part," Lisa said. "Especially if it's something we like and enjoy and want to do, even though we shouldn't. I know you're right. But there are too many things cluttering up my life. I'll have to consider my priorities before I make any decision."

"Let's go across the road to that small stream and sit down on the grass beside it to eat our lunch," Abby suggested. "This is the same spring where Elisha threw in a handful of salt to make the bad water good. It still supplies water for the gardens of Jericho.

"Jericho is a winter resort for Arabs who live in Jerusalem. It gets terribly cold up in those Judean mountains, with rain, icy winds, snow and even blizzards. Wealthy Arabs who own a place here come for weekends to rest. The town is a mixture of both Christians and Muslims.

"We're told that the religion of Mohammed was by the sword; the religion of Christ is by love. The reason Mohammed and his followers gathered momentum as they marched through the Middle East as far as Spain is because they put their swords to people's throats and shouted, 'Islam!' That word means, 'surrender,' or get your throat cut. As a result, for fear of death, the number of Muslim converts increased."

"How different Christianity is, emphasizing God's love through Christ to us. No one can force us to believe," Peter remarked. "We do use a sword, but it is the Bible, the Word of God. We surrender our will, not to a religion of works, but to a loving personal relationship of faith in God."

Following lunch and the tasty oranges for dessert, they drove along the main road leading to the Dead Sea.

"Can we swim here?" asked Megan.

"Yes, it'll be fun. You can't sink in the water because of the high salt content. It makes you float. But if you have a scratch or a cut it'll sting a little. Be careful not to get it in your mouth or eyes. Don't splash anyone. Just sit down like you're in a chair and paddle around. When we finish, we can shower with fresh water over there."

Lisa wrinkled her nose as she dipped her toes into the water. "Are you sure this is safe?" she asked hesitantly.

"Very. It's also quite sanitary, since nothing can live in it. It's pure."

"The water feels a little oily but it's so clear we can see the stones on the bottom!" Cindy said.

"Oh, I do love this!" Megan laughed. "Let's stay here forever, Colin."

"That's my wife, Merry Megan," he laughed with her.

Suddenly Lisa cried out, "Oh, Peter, I got some in my eye. Help! What shall I do? It hurts!"

Always the sympathetic doctor, Andrew responded quickly and with authority. "Get out of the water and go over to that shower. Wash your eye with the fresh water. Cindy, why don't you go with her?"

Abby was surprised that Peter did not jump out of the water and rush to Lisa's aid. *But maybe he realized this was something for Andrew to deal with. Or, perhaps he's tired of always having to help her out of scrapes, actual or imaginary. This may be his way of urging her to help herself. She certainly is able.*

As the water dried on their faces, arms and legs, a thin layer of salt appeared.

Colin licked his arm. "It really does taste like salt!" he exclaimed, "but it's a little bitter."

Megan tasted her lips. "Yes, it is salty," she laughed as she sampled some on the back of her hand.

"Better now?" asked Andrew as Cindy and Lisa joined them.

"Slightly," Lisa answered, with a reproachful glance at Peter.

After a shower to wash away the salt, they drove along the sea past a sign that read, "David's Spring."

"This is the mountain where David hid in caves when King Saul was chasing him," Abby said. "A friend of mine climbed up that path to the spring and slept there overnight. Early the next morning he was shocked to be suddenly confronted by a mountain lion! He waved and yelled and flapped his sleeping bag and it slowly retreated. After similar reports, government officials regretted having introduced the animals into that area, even though originally it was their natural habitat.

"What do you think those white chunks are in the water?" asked Abby as they stopped near the shore. "There are big ones here in front of us, too."

"They must be salt deposits," Colin guessed.

"They're like giant toadstools!" cried Megan. She quickly ran over to one, wet her finger and touched it. "They really are salt," she exclaimed, "huge, solid chunks of salt!"

She found another and sat down on top. "It's a chair!" she crowed, "and there are lots of them in all sizes! They look like snow but they're not cold. The ground is all white, too, and it crunches when we walk on it."

"Sit down for a minute," shouted Colin as he aimed the video camera in Megan's direction and then zoomed in on Cindy.

Lisa posed gracefully as he panned in her direction, and Abby admitted she looked beautiful enough for the cover of a magazine.

On the drive back, Abby pointed out Qumran. "Those caves are where part of the book of Isaiah was hidden for hundreds of years. A Bedouin boy tending his goats crawled into a cave and spied the treasure in a clay jar. Eventually it was put into a museum in Jerusalem. We'll see it when we tour the city."

"The children would love to explore those caves," said Megan.

"And would they ever love a swim in the Dead Sea!" added Colin.

Heading back toward Jerusalem, they stopped beside an old remodeled building. A sign read, "Inn of the Good Samaritan." A tent was pitched close by and a Bedouin warmly greeted the visitors.

"Come, sit down and have coffee," he urged. They followed him into the tent where he proceeded to roast a handful of coffee beans in a long-handled skillet over the fire. Then he poured them into a mortar and pounded them with a pestle.

"Each of the fifteen Bedouin tribes makes a different-sounding rhythm as they grind their coffee," Abby explained. The man emptied the powder into a brass pot filled with water and put it on a wire rack over the fire. After the coffee boiled up three times he poured it into delicate demitasse cups decorated with a camel train in gold encircling the bowl.

Again, Lisa refused to drink, and again Abby made the excuse to their host that the lady was unwell. She talked at length with the man and gave him an Arabic Bible.

Jericho

Outside, a guide showed them his camel. He said this one was his special friend. To prove it he kissed the smelly animal on its thick flabby lips!

"Ugh," said Lisa. "How could he? How revolting! Camels are dirty and they have terribly bad breath!"

"You're quite right, Lisa. But some Americans kiss their pets. Our children do, although not on the lips. I guess it's a sign of loving friendship," Colin said.

For the rest of the climb up the hills to Jerusalem and on past Bethlehem, the friends returned to their discussion of temptation.

"The key is prayer," Peter said. "Pray to recognize temptation when it comes, then pray for help to overcome it. Jesus knows and understands."

"I've never tried that approach," Lisa admitted. "Maybe it would work. I'll have to consider it tonight."

After dinner, Lisa looked for Peter but he had disappeared. Angry and sullen, she found Abby and demanded to know where he was.

"I'm not sure, but I think he is with his sister. May I help you?"

"No," Lisa laughed cynically. "You've nothing I need. I'll find him if it takes all night!"

She was waiting for him when he emerged from Julia's apartment. "Peter, let's take a walk. I know I won't be able to sleep this early."

"Sorry, Lisa, there's something I need to do. Some other time, perhaps." He hurried to his room without a further explanation. He was disturbed and needed to sort out his thoughts. Julia had just warned him about spending too much time with Lisa. She felt he should be aware of her intentions. *I'm not sure I agree with her suspicions. Her advice is well taken, yet I feel sorry for the woman and I really want to help her. Maybe Julia has misjudged the situation. However, I'll try to be more careful in the future. I don't want Lisa to get a false impression of my attentions.*

Comforting Arms

Peter knelt and poured out his heart to the Lord, asking for wisdom and clear guidance in the situation.

Lisa pouted, stamped her foot and marched off to her room, determined to have her own way and use any means at her disposal to get what she wanted.

Chapter 19

Massada

*L*isa could not sleep. Her mind kept racing over the conversation of the day.

Temptation. Overcoming. I really don't want to bother with these thoughts. They are too disturbing. I'm anxious to get out of life all I can while I'm still young enough to enjoy it. Why should I be bound by these straight-laced rules prohibiting pleasure? Yet Andrew and Cindy, and Colin and Megan seem to be having lots of fun. Haven't they ever had hardship and pain like I have? I'm going to pry into their private lives and find out.

She finally slept fitfully, woke up crabby and was late joining the group assembled for instructions. "It will be a short day but rather tiring, so we'll return early and rest up. Tomorrow we'll spend the day in Jerusalem," Abby said.

"We're cutting cross-country on our way to Massada. Right now we can catch a glimpse of Tekoa, where the prophet Amos lived and shepherded flocks."

"Look, there are more Bedouin tents," said Colin. "And one with a TV antenna sticking up."

"Yes, I've visited in that camp many times. Did I tell you what happened there?"

"Please do, even if we've already heard. We like your stories!" Megan said.

"Well, my husband and I had stopped to distribute Bibles. They invited us into the first tent and we had a nice visit with the family. They served us coffee, accepted the Bible we presented and seemed pleased.

Comforting Arms

"About a year later we returned to this same area. A sheikh met us on the road before we got to the first tent. He threatened us angrily and said, 'You came here before and left a Bible in my tent. I was not here. When I returned and found it, I burned it. Don't you ever come here again or I'll make trouble for you!'

"We were shocked. No Bedouin had ever treated us like that. They always were gracious and hospitable, even if they did not agree with our religious beliefs.

"My husband calmly said to the man, 'God loves you.' I added, 'And we love you.' I think the sheikh was so shocked he could not answer. He just turned and walked away. We drove on with heavy hearts, because there were other tents in the area we had not reached."

"So you never got to them?"

"Oh, there's a sequel to the story. After my husband died, I returned to live in Bethlehem for another four-year term of service. When a group of college students wanted to go with me to the Bedouins, I prayed about where to take them. The Lord impressed upon me the need to return to the camp near Tekoa. I told the students it might be like going into the lion's den, but God would take care of us, as He did Daniel.

"We drove up to the camp and a sheikh met us. He invited us into his tent and we had coffee together. When he smiled, I recognized him as the same man who had threatened my husband and me a few years earlier.

"He looked at me and asked, 'Have I seen you somewhere before?'

"I changed the subject quickly by asking about his family. His little grandson was ill in a hospital in Bethlehem, down the road from where I lived. I promised to visit him and send them word of his condition. I did. And after that we became the best of friends!

"The last time I went to see them, I could not find the sheikh's tent. The Bedouins said it had been moved. When I finally located it, I asked for my friend. His family told me he had died. I was shocked and saddened. I remembered one of the visits to his camp when he noticed my long skirt and headscarf, a sign of Muslim modesty. He said, 'You're a real Bedouin lady!' That warmed my heart. I was glad we had given him the gospel. By faith I believe that someday I'll see that sheikh in heaven."

"I'm sure you will, Abby," Peter said with conviction.

"We've come to the south end of the Dead Sea," Abby said as she pointed to tall dust-covered mounds. "Those are salt. The buildings here process salt and chemicals. You can see small trains loaded with bags ready to be exported. As we drive along the coast road notice how dried up the sea is. Both the countries of Jordan and Israel use the heavily laden water to extract not only salt but valuable minerals, and unfortunately it's diminishing rapidly. There is supposed to be a pillar along the way resembling Lot's wife. Some people use their imagination and say they've seen it."

"I'll find it," Megan giggled.

"Nonsense," Lisa said. "It would be long gone, melted from the weather or washed away by the rains."

"You're probably right," Megan agreed, "but it's fun to look, anyway."

"We're approaching Massada, where the Jews made their last stand against the Romans. They committed suicide rather than allow themselves to be captured and lead a life of slavery. Let's climb aboard this cable car. It'll take us near the top."

"Wait," Lisa urged. "I see a path. Why can't we climb up and save that expensive fee?"

"You can, Lisa. It would be terribly hot and exhausting, but you are welcome to try if you wish. I must warn you, though, the path is about a two-mile climb because it winds around, and it's extremely dangerous in narrow places with deep gorges on both sides."

Ignoring Abby's reply, she said, "I do wish. Peter, how about you?"

Comforting Arms

"Sorry, Lisa. I think we need to conserve our energy for investigating the ruins at the top."

"I don't advise it, Lisa," spoke up Andrew. "Dehydration can hit you quickly in this hot sun."

"Well, if you insist. You're the doctor. You should know. But I've heard of cable car accidents and I don't relish a ride in one. It looks like those deep chasms are hundreds of feet below the car. I can see it moving slowly across space. It's scary. Peter, I need you beside me."

Peter stood with her and they were off. When the car stopped, there were still steps to climb.

"Oh, no. I thought we'd be right at the top. Why didn't you tell us, Abby?"

Cindy stepped in. "It's not far. You can do it. You were going to try and climb the whole way, weren't you?"

"Never mind. I just hope all this bother is worth it." At the top she asked, "What are we supposed to see, Abby?"

"If you look over the side, there's a wall built by the Romans when they laid siege to the Jews. At the west leading to the wall is a ramp and the remains of catapults and other equipment used a few years ago by a company that made a movie of the story. Below are the old outlines of a number of Roman camps."

They began walking around the site and Abby continued, "King Herod built a wall of white stone around the top and erected thirty-eight towers on it. The plateau covers about twenty acres. At one end were storehouses holding massive quantities of food: grain, wine and dates enough to feed men for a long time. Weapons of war were stored there, too."

"You mentioned King Herod?"

"Yes, he also built an extensive palace with floors of beautiful colored stones, high strong walls and elaborate baths. Here are the remains. A royal bathing pool was cut out of the rock. Huge reservoirs assured him of an adequate water supply, even for planting gardens."

Massada

"What a setup!" commented Colin. "The old boy sure looked after himself. We saw where he was buried in Herodion. But he left it all behind. Wealth is useless when we die. And these Jews were dead when the Romans finally broke through their fortifications?"

"Yes. The Jews chose ten men to slay everyone else, and then cast lots for one man to kill them as they lay with their arms around their wives and children. The last man was to commit suicide. Altogether, there were nine hundred and sixty. It was the last stronghold of the Jewish Revolt. It took the Romans three years of siege to finally capture the place."

An hour's tramp in the hot sun was sufficient for them to see the ruins. "Let's catch the next cable car and then have a cool drink down below," Abby suggested.

"Did I hear you correctly? A cool drink? I can't believe it! Let's go!" Lisa's lethargy disappeared and she needed no arm to lean on as she hurried down the steps.

"I'm sorry," she apologized with a sweet smile as she rushed to be first in the cable car, pushing ahead of people waiting in line. At a souvenir shop she purchased a T-shirt and postcards.

Sam was waiting in the parking lot. Everyone was glad to return to the guest home, shower and relax after a late lunch. Colin and Megan started a Scrabble game in the lounge. Andrew and Cindy chose books to read from the well-stocked library that covered the length of an entire wall.

"Where's Peter?" Lisa asked as she stood in the archway and scanned the room.

"I believe he's gone for a walk with Julia," Abby answered.

"Oh. Well, I need someone to talk to. Megan, come sit beside me."

Megan smiled at her husband and left the game. She knew he understood. They both sensed Lisa's need and silently prayed for wisdom.

The two women walked to one end of the lounge and sat down, lowering their voices for privacy.

Comforting Arms

"Megan, tell me how you and Colin manage to appear so happy together."

"We work at it, Lisa. No marriage can survive without a lot of giving and forgiving."

"Stop right there. That I could never do. Once hurt, that's the end. I can't tolerate offenses. Forgive? Never!"

"But when you love someone, you accept them as they are, with their faults and foibles. You can't try to change them into what you think they should be. No one is perfect."

"You're wrong. My husband did change. He swore he would not touch liquor if I married him. And he didn't. But when he began staying out late at night and coming home drunk he broke his vow to me. I can never forgive him for that. I guess you've not had to deal with that kind of emotional pain."

"There you're quite wrong. We did have a serious problem. Perhaps it will help if I tell you about it. Colin was a workaholic. He was gone for days at a time on business trips. As a result, he neglected his family. Our communications were at a standstill. We drifted apart. I was deeply concerned and I did not want to see our marriage disintegrate. I prayed and you know, sometimes faith without works is dead! I decided to do something about it. I made an appointment with his secretary for a time to see him in his office. He was surprised when I walked in and said we needed to talk and this was the only way we could find time to do it."

"So. There you have it. Why didn't you leave him?"

"Because I loved him. We talked it over. I tried to understand his point of view. He gave the usual excuse that he was working hard to make money for us. I assured him that we would rather have his love than his money! That simple but profound statement opened his eyes. He begged me to forgive him and I did. He had been gone so much that he hardly knew his two children. Now he proves he loves us by spending quality time with us every weekend. God has blessed us with a unique compatibility and joy that few marriages can equal."

"Well, that story is hard to believe. I never could do what you did."

"It took a lot of prayer and wisdom. But it was worth it. I have my family and my husband's love and support. God has blessed us in many ways and we are thankful."

Lisa stood up abruptly. "I'm puzzled and confused. How could you do it?"

"Only by relying on God's grace and wisdom and strength, certainly none of my own. But I trusted Him and He provided all I needed. Christ lives within my heart."

"Incredible." Lisa walked over to Cindy, took the book out of her hand and ordered, "Come, let's go to the rose arbor and sit down. I want to talk to you."

Cindy complied reluctantly. But like Megan, she knew Lisa was troubled and needed counseling.

"Tell me, Cindy, you are always calm and unperturbed by whatever happens. How do you do it?"

"I'll tell you, Lisa. Andrew and I have had our problems. I nearly left him after our baby was born prematurely and died. I was devastated and I could not conquer my grief. We knew that I was unable to have another child and I felt Andrew deserved to have the family he wanted. I loved him too much to deny him that pleasure. He returned from the hospital one day to find me packing, ready to leave."

"Oh, that's ridiculous. No woman would make that kind of sacrifice if she were in love. Tough luck for Andrew."

"No, Lisa. I really meant to set him free. But he wouldn't hear of it. He took me to a wise minister who counseled us both. We are in the process of adopting a baby now and I believe this is all a part of God's plan for us. Some tiny child needs the love and Christian guidance we can provide. We're very happy about it. We've let God control our lives and He can do a much better job of it than we can.

Comforting Arms

I've learned that committing my life to Christ, who lives within my heart, is the only way to experience true joy. This is why I can remain calm."

"You and Megan both talk about Christ living within. How so?"

"You just ask Him. Tell Him you're sorry for your sin, ask His forgiveness and open your heart so that His Spirit may live within you and be your guide in all you think and say and do."

"That's all?"

"Yes. But that's just the beginning. Then you read the Bible, His Word, because that's how He speaks to you. And you speak to Him in prayer."

"I don't know if I can do that. It's a big decision. I've done a lot of wrong things and made a lot of stupid decisions. He'd have a big job trying to change me! Now I want to find Peter."

She didn't find him. So she went to her room to think about what she had heard. Some of it was hard to believe and she was not sure she could resist the temptation to arrange things the way she wanted them to be. But she was game to try anything.

Peter was having tea with his sister in her apartment. Again, Julia warned him about his relationship with Lisa. "Please be careful, dear. We know you mean well, but your kindness to her can easily be misconstrued. I'm seriously concerned because I love you."

"Thanks, Julia. I appreciate your loving care. You do understand. I promise to heed your warning." As he was leaving the apartment he collided with Abby.

"I beg your pardon," Peter said politely.

"I'm so sorry to be late for tea," Abby apologized. "Julia asked me to come but Sam needed advice about the trip to Jerusalem tomorrow."

"Please come in, and you, too, Peter. We can chat while Abby has her tea," Julia said as she put the kettle back on. "What are your plans following this tour, Abby? Why don't you stay here with me for a while? Do you need to fly back with the rest of the group?"

"No, not necessarily. They can manage quite well on their own. And I could use a few days of relaxation. Your offer is tempting."

Peter spoke up. "Adnan, in Joppa, asked me to come and preach in his church after this tour ended. I hope you will go with me."

"Right. I haven't forgotten. I'll arrange for it and for some of the other churches, too," Abby answered.

"Good. It's settled then. You both will be my guests," Julia said with satisfaction. "Now I need to see about dinner." She quickly left, hoping Peter would take advantage of the opportunity to be with Abby.

"I think my sister is trying to be a matchmaker," Peter grinned.

As she stood up Abby replied, "You're probably right, but perhaps discretion is advisable. Please excuse me, Peter. I think I should leave."

"I understand. But let me tell you how much I appreciate you and all you have done. I admire you tremendously." He came and stood close to her, and as his eyes met hers they sparkled with a bright light. He took both of her hands in his, held them firmly, then with a warm squeeze, released them.

Abby went to her room. Her heart was light with thoughts of Peter and their arrangements for after the tour ended. Yet there was a nagging reminder of Lisa and what God's plans might be for her.

Chapter 20

Jerusalem

The group left the West Bank and traveled down the main road. "There are many things to see in Jerusalem," Abby said. "Those big homes on your left used to belong to wealthy Arabs. When Israel became a nation in 1948, the Jews took them over and the Arabs were turned out, some of them fleeing with only what they could carry. Refugee camps were set up. In fact, there is one not far from where we're staying. You may have noticed it, enclosed in barbed wire. Often a curfew is imposed by the Israelis if there's been stoning, rioting or fighting."

"Now we understand why the Bible mentions stoning as punishment. There are stones everywhere! This country seems to be in a continuous state of war, each side vehemently retaliating for offenses committed by the other," Andrew said.

"Precisely. If only they could settle their differences amicably. But I'm afraid that won't happen until Jesus, the Prince of Peace, comes.

"We're passing over the Valley of Hinnom. It was used for idol worship and child sacrifice. Jeremiah wrote about it and said people burned their sons and daughters in the fire in the valley of slaughter. King Ahaz did this, too, copying the abominations of the heathen whom the Lord had cast out. It was a place of depravity and wickedness. I'm sorry our day is beginning with unpleasant sites but we'll finish on a happier note."

Jerusalem

"I certainly hope so, Abby. What a gloomy way to start," was Lisa's curt comment.

"Here we are at the Holocaust museum. It's a memorial to the six million Jews who perished in Europe at the time of the Second World War. There's a lot of evidence relating to the catastrophe, and the names of the death camps are listed. I've been through it once and I cannot face the terrible things on display. It's sad beyond description. Lisa, you may find it difficult. If you'd like to stay in the van with me, please do."

"Oh, I'll go in. Peter will be with me, won't you, Peter? I won't need to face any difficult situation alone, as long as he's beside me."

"Of course, Lisa. If you wish."

"I do wish."

The group returned, subdued and shaken. Lisa looked pale. Megan was in tears. Cindy shook her head in despair. The men were quiet.

"Now for a more cheerful note. We're on our way to The Shrine of the Book. Seven priceless Dead Sea Scrolls are housed here. Along with the book of Isaiah and other manuscripts is the commentary of Habakkuk. They are all kept carefully enclosed in a controlled temperature for preservation. Remember, when we went to the Dead Sea we saw the caves of Qamran where the scrolls were found."

"Isn't it awesome how God caused these parts of His Word to be preserved?" Peter said as they viewed the scrolls. "It certainly confirms our faith."

"That it does," agreed Abby. "Next we'll wade through Hezekiah's Tunnel, quite a feat of engineering you'll enjoy, Colin. King Hezekiah's workmen chipped through solid rock to make a conduit one thousand seven hundred and eighty feet long in order to divert the spring of Gihon. The men hacked their way through from each end and met in the middle! This provided the water supply for Jerusalem and at the same time protected it from enemy attack.

"Take off your sneakers or sandals, everyone. The water will be up to our knees in some places, and in others the tunnel is so narrow we'll have to stoop over a little. Be careful not to slip."

"Peter, here we go again. I'll hang onto you."

"That may be difficult, Lisa. We have to go single file."

They all emerged smiling except Lisa. "I won't go through that kind of punishment again. You should have warned me, Abby. How can you subject us to such rough treatment? And it's way past lunchtime. Haven't you any idea of the energy we've expended in all this sightseeing?"

Abby breathed a quick sentence prayer for God to keep her calm and prevent her from answering as she wanted to.

"As we climb these steps, look back at the pool formed at the tunnel's exit. It's called the Pool of Siloam. Jesus told a blind man to wash in that pool. When he obeyed, he was healed.

"We're on our way to lunch right now, Lisa. I've arranged for us to eat at a little shop managed by one of my Arab friends. Here we are. Meet Tony, everyone. He makes the best falafels in town. You add your own choice of salads into the pocket-bread. They are homemade and tasty. There are onions, chopped cucumbers, shredded cabbage, tomatoes, a hot spicy sauce and salad dressing made of beaten sesame seeds, one of my favorites."

"Soft drinks are on the house for you," Tony offered. "We have the samples you see over there: Coke, Pepsi, 7-Up and Orange Crush. Choose what you like."

"That's very generous of you, my friend," Peter said.

"What in the world is a falafel?" Lisa asked. "Are you sure it's safe?"

"It's made of ground chickpeas mixed with a number of spices, formed into a patty and deep-fried. It's the equivalent of an American hamburger, quite nutritious and delicious," Abby answered. "Try one."

Jerusalem

"I'm hungry enough to eat anything," Lisa sighed, and piled her sandwich thick with salads.

"After we finish eating, our next stop will be the Temple Mount," Abby announced. "On our way, we'll stop to climb through a little wooden door built within a big one. It's called, 'the eye of the needle.' It opens onto a private neighborhood where a friend of mine lives. People use the small door now, but in the old days when camels brought supplies, the larger one had to be opened."

One at a time they stepped through the small opening onto a cemented area. Steps led up to apartments and Abby's friend, Huda, came to greet her. After introductions, Huda invited the group for coffee and with nods of approval from the couples, Abby accepted. Their visit was brief but enlightening as Huda explained in English that the adjacent church was named for St. John because it is believed to be where he was beheaded.

They thanked Huda for her kind hospitality and as they climbed back through the 'eye of the needle' Peter remarked, "I can see why Jesus said it's harder for a rich man to enter heaven, than for a camel to get through this tiny door. It would need to have its burdens unloaded! Even then, it would be virtually impossible. But with God, nothing is impossible."

"Why do we have to walk so far?" grumbled Lisa as she tripped over a cobblestone and then quickly dodged a donkey carrying a load of vegetables. Peter caught her both times as she nearly fell.

Abby did not reply to the constant comments. She knew Lisa could not be tired and certainly not that clumsy, just aching for attention and sympathy.

At the Temple Mount, a holy Muslim site, Abby said, "Notice the massive blocks of white marble and the multicolored mosaics. The gold dome glistens in the sunlight and you can see it from long distances away. The beautiful Arabic script decorating the mosque is quotations from the Koran in praise of Mohammed. It is said that he came here

Comforting Arms

mounted on his favorite mare before he ascended into heaven.

"The original temple was built by King Solomon close by, although not directly beneath as scholars thought formerly. A few years ago, ruins believed to be from the first temple were discovered underground a short distance away. We cannot see them because angry Muslims closed up the passageway. They control the property. Whenever Jews try to enter the Temple Mount, violent fighting erupts.

"King Herod erected a new, even more beautiful building that was later destroyed. The Romans set up a temple to their god Jupiter and put in statues of their emperors. When the Arabs came to Jerusalem after their conquest of Palestine, Omar made it a house of worship. Later, a Muslim ruler built this present one. The Crusaders converted it into a church and when they were defeated, the Muslim conquerors turned it into a shrine. It's considered the second most holy place in Islam. The Muslims gather for prayers every Friday. Before they enter, they sit on these little stone chairs in front of the water faucets and wash their arms, hands, legs and feet according to prescribed ritual.

"We have to take off our shoes before we enter the mosque. Here inside, the rugs are used for kneeling to pray, and the lectern in front is where the priest gives his sermon. That big rock with the chain hanging above is believed to be how Mohammed climbed to heaven. Beside it is a box supposedly containing a few hairs from his beard. The stone may also be the place where Abraham offered up Isaac.

"Through that opening are steps leading to a subterranean cave. The Muslims believe that the souls of the dead assemble there to pray. They say Elijah, King David, Solomon and Mohammed prayed there."

"This must be the Wailing Wall," remarked Peter as they left and walked down an outside ramp. They passed huge, thick slabs of stones. Jewish men stood rhythmically bumping their foreheads against the stones.

"They're swaying back and forth like they did on the

Jerusalem

plane when we were flying to Tel Aviv," remarked Megan. "You told us they were praying."

"Yes," Abby said. "Some of the wall is down below the ground and probably dates from King Solomon's original building of the Temple. It has been destroyed and rebuilt and the Jews consider it their holiest shrine. People write prayers on little pieces of paper and tuck them into the cracks between the stones, hoping God will see and answer them. You can even fax a prayer to the telephone company, pay a fee and they will print out your prayer, bring it here and tuck it into the wall."

"Do they really believe God sees those notes and will answer them?" queried Lisa.

"Yes. We know He understands and He will answer according to His purpose.

"Young recruits to the Israeli army are brought here to take an oath of allegiance. It's said that God's Divine Presence rests eternally upon this Wailing Wall. Legend tells us that in the dead of night a white dove representing God's Presence appears and coos comfortingly with those who mourn. Drops of dew that cover the stones are the tears of the Wailing Wall, shed with weeping Israel."

"Nonsense," muttered Lisa. "How can they believe such ridiculous stories?"

Abby did not reply. *It's useless to try and explain anything. Best I keep quiet. Let her believe what she likes.*

"Now we're at the end of the Wailing Wall, and we'll walk through this long tunnel underneath the Old City. It was discovered only a few years ago. Kings used to ride in their chariots along that wide wall. Fascinating, isn't it? Shops do a thriving business like they must have done in Old Testament times. But I warn you, these items are extremely costly because the merchants cater to the tourists."

In spite of the warning, Lisa decided to shop here and there, making the group wait while she took her time deciding what she wanted.

"Come on, Lisa, you're holding us up," Colin urged.

"Well, I've waited for you all lots of times. Now you can return the favor." She emerged from the third shop wearing a gorgeous silk scarf in rainbow colors tied around her shoulders. It enhanced her luminous eyes and the sheen of her soft, silky hair.

"Wow," breathed Colin and Andrew together.

Peter thought, *Yes, she certainly looks gorgeous on the outside. But oh, the inside!*

Lord, give me patience, Abby prayed, and said, "I think we've had enough for one day. Let's head home. Tomorrow we'll see more of this Old City and do some shopping."

As they turned a corner and approached one of the main streets, a strange cloud of white smoke appeared just ahead. "Quickly, duck into this shop before the doors are closed," shouted Abby.

The two couples and Peter obediently hurried inside but Lisa lingered to see why people were running into every open door they could find.

"Lisa, please hurry. Come on!" Abby grabbed her arm and tried to drag her into the shop. She resisted violently, pulling away and complaining, "I'll not be dictated to by you or anyone else! I want to see what's happening."

Soldiers in full combat uniform dashed past with their guns ready. At the sound of gunshots Lisa finally decided to move, but not before the smoke nearly engulfed her. She began coughing violently and rushed into the shop, her face white with fear. "What...happened?" she blurted out between gasps.

"I tried to warn you. I'm sorry you inhaled some of that tear gas, Lisa. Try to exhale as much as you can. There must have been a riot near here and the army used gas to disperse the demonstrators."

"My eyes...nose...mouth...throat...are on fire. I...think...I'm going to...pass out." Her legs buckled and she began to fall. Andrew caught her and helped her to a chair. The storekeeper brought a glass of water.

"I've got...a terrible...headache. I think I'm...going to be sick. I feel...wretched."

"Take it easy for a few minutes. Tear gas is meant to frighten its victims so they won't cause any more trouble. You may feel the effects for a while but they'll wear off," Andrew assured her.

"I'll never forgive you...for bringing us...into this...situation," she gasped between breaths. "I'm going to sue you...for personal injury, Abby. My health may be ruined... permanently, for all I know."

"Oh, Lisa, be sensible," Colin said. "Abby did the best she could under this unavoidable circumstance. She warned you, remember."

"Take deep breaths, Lisa," Andrew said. "You'll be alright."

"As soon as the way is clear we can head home. We've had enough for one day," Abby decided.

"I don't think I can walk. Peter, you'll have to carry me."

Before the object of her affection could make a move, Andrew swept her up in his arms, and with Cindy helping, carried her to the van where Sam had it waiting. Lisa began her usual antagonistic comments, but Colin interrupted her by saying, "Stop it, Lisa. That's enough. No one wants to hear your complaints. Leave Abby alone."

Lisa did not appear for dinner. Cindy offered to take her the tray Julia prepared, relieving Abby of the dreaded encounter.

"Where is Abby?" Lisa asked as she lay propped up in bed. "Why hasn't she come to apologize?"

"She's finishing dinner. I've brought yours." Cindy plumped the pillows and then beat a hasty exit to avoid more of Lisa's cutting criticism of Abby.

Peter was relieved that Lisa did not appear for dinner. He found Abby and asked her to join him for a walk. "I'm sorry, Peter. I would be happy to come with you but I promised Sam I would teach his wife how to make some special cookies. Another time, perhaps?"

"Right. You're always helping someone. Bless you. Good night."

Chapter 21

The Old City Gates

Lisa was late for breakfast and announced, "I'm too upset to do anything today. You'll have to go without me. Peter, stay with me. I want to talk with you."

"I'm sorry, Lisa. I can't miss seeing more of Jerusalem. This is important to me. I'm sure Julia will take good care of you while we're gone."

"We're going to do some shopping," offered Cindy. "You don't want to miss that opportunity, do you?"

"Well, I guess not. After all, I paid enough for this trip. I might as well get the most for my money." Lisa hurriedly drank a cup of coffee, grabbed some toast and joined the others in the waiting van.

As they approached Jerusalem, Abby said, "Notice the thick walls surrounding the old city. Soldiers still crouch behind the slits in the crenellated battlements where arrows were shot down upon advancing enemies. Now they shoot guns from there.

"The entire city is enclosed with walls, and it can only be entered when the gates are open. During fighting, they're closed so terrorists can be rooted out. Some of the tremendous slabs of stone probably date back to Nehemiah's time of rebuilding or even earlier.

"We're walking through Zion Gate. It leads to Mount Zion where we're headed. Those pockmarks in the cement pillars are the results of stray bullets shot during Jewish-Arab fighting in 1948.

"Here is King David's tomb, honored by both the Jews and the Muslims. Now let's go on to the Upper Room where Jesus and His disciples participated in the Last Supper. It's a good place to meditate about what happened there. I've asked Peter to read the Scripture story and pray."

"This is a special place reminding us of communion which we celebrate in church. Our part is to be worthy of what Jesus did for us on the cross."

"And how, pray tell, are we made worthy?" Lisa's voice was tinged with her ever-present bitterness.

"Simply by accepting Jesus' provision of forgiveness for our sins. We only have to ask Him, and we receive it by faith," Peter explained.

"Well, it sounds too easy. Seems to me we need to earn His forgiveness. We have to do good things, go to church, give money, be philanthropists."

"That can't be done, no matter how hard we try. Our works are never good enough when they are weighed against our faults and failures."

"So what's the use of trying?"

"We don't have to try. It was done for us on the cross."

"Here we go again. The cross. Leave it right there."

"Yes, exactly. Leave your sin there. Let Jesus forgive and make you a new person."

"That's what you keep saying."

"We'll walk back toward the market and shop if you like," Abby said." I don't recommend that you buy anything to eat that cannot be peeled or shelled. There are interesting items and souvenirs in many of the shops. Let's stick together. It's easy to get lost in this maze of narrow streets. It's also easy to get your pocket picked or your purse stolen, so hold on to your valuables."

"Look out, Megan. Here comes a crowd of people. Let's back up against this wall!" warned Colin. But the warning was too late. Just as Megan turned, the crowd surged past and bumped her from behind. If Colin had not reached out his strong arms to catch her, she would have fallen pell-mell down the stone steps.

"Whew, that was close," she laughed. But before she could collect her wits, a man pushing a cart brushed against her. Again she lost her balance and again Colin rescued her from another fall.

"Are you all right, Megan?" Abby asked.

"Right as rain," she answered cheerily. "Oh, look at that gorgeous long dress. It's embroidered in beautiful silver and gold designs. I love it."

"You shall have it," Colin responded, and promptly haggled over the price. "I know I probably paid too much for it. But there you are, my dear. A reward for taking this all in your stride with no complaining."

"Your sarcasm is lost on me, Colin," Lisa remarked. "All I want to do is get out of this dumpy Old City." She stopped abruptly. "Oh, I've changed my mind. Over there's something I've just got to have. Wait for me!"

They stopped while she purchased a filmy blouse. She was still holding her wallet when the shopkeeper raised his arm up high in the air with her money in his hand.

"What in the world is he doing?" Lisa asked, wondering about his strange behavior.

Quickly a man emerged from the crowd of shoppers, grabbed the money out of the merchant's hand and went on down the street.

Lisa was astonished. "What's going on?" she frowned disapproval.

"It's all right," grinned the shopkeeper. "He's a friend of mine."

Assuming it didn't matter, she turned and hurried to rejoin the group up ahead. They passed several shops displaying more beautiful gowns, antiques and jewelry.

Lisa stopped to look. "Oh, I must have that necklace," she chortled, and picked out an exquisite gold chain with a pendant of diamonds and rubies. She reached into her purse and abruptly stood still.

Comforting Arms

"Wait. There's something wrong. I thought I put my wallet back into my purse. But I can't find it!" She rummaged around, searching.

Abby and friends waited patiently.

"I'm sure I put it back into my purse after I bought that blouse." Her voice was shaking. "But it isn't here."

"Let me look," Cindy offered. She took the purse and made a thorough search. "You're quite right. That wallet is not here."

Lisa turned to Abby. "What shall I do? You've put me in this situation. It's your fault. Now get me back my wallet, pronto!"

"Let's go back to that shop," Abby decided.

"Sir," she motioned to the shopkeeper, "this lady bought a blouse here just a few minutes ago and now her wallet is missing."

"I don't know anything about it," he replied nonchalantly.

"But we were right here. She gave you the money."

"Are you accusing me of stealing?"

"Well, now the wallet is gone."

"So go tell the police."

"All right, we will." Abby led her friends back up the steps toward the Arab Police Station.

"That man probably thinks we're all tourists. He doesn't know I lived in the West Bank and speak Arabic. We'll report this and see what happens."

At the Station, Abby explained their predicament. The officer in charge pulled out a form and ordered Lisa to fill it in, listing all of the items contained in the wallet.

He glanced at the address Lisa wrote. "You're staying in the West Bank?"

"Yes," Abby answered in Arabic. "I know the shop where the wallet was stolen."

"You speak Arabic! All right, we'll send a detective with you to the shop."

"Peter, come with me," Lisa begged.

Abby, Peter and Lisa went with the detective.

"This lady's wallet was stolen here," the detective said to the shopkeeper. "Come along." Reluctantly, the man obeyed.

They returned to the station and the irate merchant yelled, "I am innocent. I did not steal your wallet. How can you say this? You are wrong. I did not do it. I'm not a thief!"

Abby held her ground. "But it was right in front of your shop." She repeated how it was done, with the two men working together to distract Lisa.

"We know where the pickpockets throw the empty wallets," said the officer. "We'll call you if we find it."

"Thank you," Abby said, and they left.

"Well, thanks for nothing!" Lisa groaned. "They'll never get it back. It's gone, and a lot of money was in it. Now what shall I do?"

"We can help you out, Lisa. Don't worry," Peter comforted.

"Oh, will you? Thanks, Peter." *Well, she decided, if this brings him one step closer to me, it's worth losing the money. I've paid a lot more for other things I wanted. After all, this is going to turn out for my benefit. I'm glad it happened!*

They joined the rest of the team and Abby led them past David's Tower. "This is called the Citadel of David. You can see the remains of the moat that surrounded it. Actually, it was a large fortress, built on the site where Herod had a palace. It was one of the main fortifications guarding Jerusalem at the time the Jews revolted against Rome.

"Now we're walking through Jaffa Gate. It was built by Suleiman and marked the beginning of the road to the coast. Historians tell us that through it British troops entered in 1917 and defeated the Turks without a shot being fired. General Allenby was leading the army and when the Muslims heard his name, they misinterpreted it to mean 'bey Allah,' 'God's servant.' They thought He had sent the Englishman. So they surrendered peacefully.

"Some of these gates had a special meaning and use in Bible times. We can talk about them when we get back to the guest home. There were ten gates originally but now eight are being used. Here's our van. Sam will drive us around the Old City and I'll point out each gate."

"New Gate was opened by order of a Turkish Sultan to accommodate Christians who were living in that quarter of the Old City. There are four distinct quarters: Christian, Muslim, Armenian and Jewish."

"Armenian?" questioned Peter.

"Yes. When the people of Armenia were being persecuted by the Turks in the late 1800s, they fled by the thousands and many of them settled here in Jerusalem's Old City.

"Damascus Gate marks the beginning of the highway leading to Syria's capital. Peter, will you tell us about the original ones after dinner tonight? You probably taught their history to your students."

"You're right, Abby. I'll be glad to."

"Herod's Gate used to be the meeting place for Arabs to sell or trade their animals. Some of them still buy and sell there. We're going around now to Lions' Gate, also called St. Stephen's Gate, thought to be where he was martyred, and where Jesus made His triumphal entry into Jerusalem. On Palm Sunday each year, Arab and Jewish Christians from all over the land carry palm branches and sing as they march from the Mount of Olives, across the valley and through Stephen's Gate.

"We're driving around that same valley and from here you can see the Golden Gate. It was closed by the Muslims because of a legend stemming from Bible prophecy that says Jesus, the Prince of Peace, will return through this gate. Next is Dung Gate, where garbage and trash is carried out for disposal. And finally Zion Gate, where we entered this morning."

The Old City Gates

Outside the Old City, in New Jerusalem, they lunched at an outdoor café. Then Sam deposited them in front of an iron gate on a busy street.

"Here is a famous guest home, a historic building protected by the Israeli Government. We'll meet the manager and have a brief tour."

A kindly woman met them at the gate and led them up wide, curved steps to the large sanctuary. "This building was planned originally to be used as a church and a Bible School. The story of how it was built is unique."

"Tell us about it, please. I'm a civil engineer and I'm keenly interested," Colin said.

"You see, the missionary had an architect draw up plans. The blueprints and request for permission to build had to be sent to the Emperor in Constantinople, because the Turks were ruling the country at that time. It was the early 1900s. The Emperor refused to sign the papers because the building was to be used as a church. Muslims did not want the competition of a Christian church. The missionary was disappointed and extremely perplexed. He believed this was God's plan, so he prayed and he asked many people to pray.

"One day the Turkish official knocked on the Mission door. He was smiling as he said, 'I got permission for you to build your church.'

"The missionary was amazed. 'How did you manage to do it?'

"'Well, you're going to have a baptistry installed the church, aren't you?'

"'Yes,' the missionary replied.

"'I got permission for you to build a Turkish bath!'"

"What a story! God answered the prayers of those people in an awesome way. He certainly 'makes the wrath of man to praise Him,' doesn't He!" Peter grinned.

"This large sanctuary has served various groups over the years. Later the rest of the building became a guest home. We have a number of rooms, with two kitchens so guests can prepare their own meals. The large basement is used as a bomb shelter for the neighborhood. Let's go down to the lounge. Refreshments are ready for you."

"Ah, how comfortable," sighed Colin as he sank down on a thick sofa and patted the seat beside him for Megan. "Just what we need, exactly when we need it!"

Andrew spied the organ and with an approving glance from Abby, sat down to play. He was gifted and soon they all joined in singing, "Blest be the tie that binds our hearts in Christian love; the fellowship of kindred minds is like to that above."

"Thank you for these lovely refreshments," Abby said as they departed.

Following dinner, Lisa announced, "It has been too long and exhausting a day, Abby. You've worn us out. And I'm completely devastated about my wallet. I had more than fifty dollars in it. I'm going to bed but I probably won't sleep. I'll just toss and turn and worry." She glanced at Peter, her blue eyes pleading for sympathy. But he was deep in conversation with his sister and unaware of her appeal. She frowned and hurried away, looking back repeatedly.

The rest of the group gathered in the lounge and Peter explained the meaning of the ancient gates of Jerusalem from the book of Nehemiah.

"First is the Sheep Gate. Lambs were brought for sacrifice through it. The significance is that we are like sheep gone astray but Christ, the Lamb of God, sacrificed Himself for us.

"Next is the Fish Gate, where people entered the market to buy or sell fish. Jesus said, 'Follow me, and I will make you fishers of men.' Once we accept Christ as our personal Savior, we are to be witnesses of the experience by telling others about Him.

"Third is the Old Gate, representing our doctrinal foundation laid by the prophets and apostles. We need to be firmly established in God's Word.

"The Valley Gate teaches us humility, an attitude of the heart. There is no room for pride, which stems from the self-life. Our attitude should be, 'not I, but Christ.'

"Through the Dung Gate, refuse to be disposed of was carried out. We must examine ourselves to see if we harbor any kind of trash in thought, word or deed that needs to be cleansed away.

"The Fountain Gate suggests that the person of the Holy Spirit fills us as we surrender ourselves to Christ. Then from within us will flow life-giving water to others.

"The Water Gate tells us that the Word of God is for our spiritual cleansing from the daily defilements of sin. This is a part of our progressive spiritual life, our growth as Christians.

"Number eight is the Horse Gate. Horses were used in battle. In Christian warfare we resist the enemy, Satan, in the strength of the Lord who provides victory.

"Next comes the East Gate, called the Golden Gate, facing the Mount of Olives. As Abby told us, it is said that Jesus may return through this same gate. Believing the tradition that a Christian conqueror would someday enter through the gate and subdue his enemies, the Muslims closed the gate to prevent His coming. Some day it will be opened by the Prince of Peace to establish His kingdom, according to the prophet Ezekiel.

"The tenth is called the Gate of Miphkad. Some scholars say it was where the court of private judgment solved personal matters. Boaz settled Ruth's matter of inheritance there. Others translate it as a 'place of recruitment.' I like that explanation because it urges us to be witnesses for Christ by imploring others to accept Him. This is a missionary challenge we do well to heed. It might also represent the place of rewards for the quality of work done by believers.

"The Sheep Gate is mentioned again, pointing out that Christ is the beginning and end of our Christian experience. Each of the gates shows a progression in our life of faith and is a spiritual lesson for believers."

"Thank you, Peter, for that brief and meaningful explanation," Andrew said.

"What a challenge for us!" agreed Colin.

The couples retired and Abby walked slowly outside to meditate. She sat down on the log where Peter had found her before and thought of their conversation. *Was his only a passing interest? A means of making conversation? Or is he the one God has sent to fill the void in my heart? To hold me in his comforting arms? I need to be certain this is the Lord's doing and not my own desire for companionship.*

Her thoughts were abruptly interrupted by Peter's deep voice asking, "May I join you?"

Abby's eyes lit with pleasure as she answered, "Please do."

They sat quietly for a few moments, content in each other's company. Then Abby said, "I'm terribly sorry about the theft of Lisa's wallet."

"But I distinctly remember that you did warn us to be careful. Perhaps God has a lesson in it to teach Lisa."

"Yes, that's possible. It remains to be seen."

"You're bearing her barbed criticisms with patience. I admire you for it."

"Thank you, Peter. You must be praying for me. It's been difficult. Sometimes I've wanted to reply with a vengeance. But the others have intervened for me!"

"I'm sorry I haven't, Abby. As I explained the other night, I've been trying to help Lisa see herself and make a definite commitment to Christ. But she's determined to pursue her own interests, at least at this point, anyway. Tell me, have you firmed up our plans following the end of this tour?"

"Since you're prepared to stay, I've been arranging for you to speak to the Christians in Joppa, Nazareth, Tiberius, Jerusalem, Jericho and Bethlehem."

"That sounds great. You've been busy! Thank you, Abby."

"Julia has been helping with the details. She's a dear."

"You two are like sisters, aren't you?"

"Yes. We work together smoothly."

Abby wanted to prolong the conversation but she felt it was wise to retire. She stood up, and again Peter caught her hand and held it gently as they walked back to the guest home. With a firm squeeze he released it and said goodnight.

Chapter 22

Ein Karim

The next morning a very subdued Lisa came to the breakfast table. She looked haggard and pale in spite of the application of cosmetics. There were dark circles under her puffy blue eyes. Mascara and concealer could not hide the ravages of anxiety and sleeplessness.

She ate quietly and did not complain about the food or accommodations. Abby was shocked, amazed, bewildered and slightly relieved. *I can hardly believe this is the same woman. What in the world has happened? Am I no longer the prey for her target practice? Will there be no more barbed, poisonous arrows aimed at me? This seems like a miracle. It appears that perhaps our prayers are being answered! Mine not to question how or why, just thank God for whatever it is He is doing.*

"Did you sleep well, Lisa?" asked Andrew.

"No. I was terribly upset by the theft of my wallet. A very dear friend gave it to me on my birthday. It was expensive, soft blue leather with my embossed initials. It could never be replaced. I had to do some thinking. I might as well tell you all about it. I tossed and turned and was so angry with those two men working in cahoots that I couldn't sleep. I kept trying to think of some way to get even. That's what I've always done. Take revenge. But I couldn't think of a thing. I was afraid of doing something in this country that might get me into trouble.

"Then God started to talk to me. I didn't want to listen but He kept reminding me of how Jesus died on the cross and what He said: 'Father, forgive them, for they know not what they do.' Jesus said this about his enemies. You all had talked about forgiveness. I knew this was what I needed to do but I rebelled. I did not want to forgive those evil men. I felt violated. They had no right to take my personal property.

"I couldn't stand it any longer so I finally capitulated and said, 'Father, forgive those two men, even though they knew exactly what they were doing!' Then I felt peace and went to sleep."

The friends could not help but smile at Lisa's way of forgiving her enemies. "God understands the thoughts and sincerity of our hearts," Peter reminded them. "I'm glad you're learning to forgive, Lisa. It's a good beginning toward understanding how much God has forgiven each one of us."

"We're happy for you, Lisa. And we're praying your wallet will be returned," Abby added. "Meanwhile I'll be glad to give you money for whatever you need."

"We'll all chip in," Peter added, and the couples nodded agreement.

"Thanks. But I don't need your money. I have plenty; in fact, I've got more than I can ever use."

"Now we're ready to see a bit more of the country," Abby said.

Their road wound down into a neat terraced valley filled with olive trees and vineyards.

"Ein Karim is the birthplace of John the Baptist. Notice the lovely fountain in the middle of this small village. There are lots of churches and monasteries here. Under the Church of St. John are the remains of an arch over the entrance to the grotto where it is believed he was born. Let's go down. Here is an inscription in Latin that says, 'Blessed be the Lord God of Israel, for He hath visited and redeemed His people'. That marble slab names John as the forerunner of Christ. Those are scenes picturing his life.

"Let's go outside. Beside the road is the spring giving the village its name. Ein means spring and Karim means precious. An inscription on the wall quotes Isaiah: 'Ho, every one that thirsteth, come ye for water.'

"Here is the Church of the Visitation. It is supposedly built over the house belonging to Elizabeth and Zacharias, where Mary visited. The square design on our left is thought to represent the breastplate worn by the priests who officiated in the Holy Temple. Zacharias probably wore one similar to that."

They returned to the van and Abby said, "We'll drive north to Timnath, the city and burial place of Joshua. Peter, will you give us a brief outline of his life while we travel?"

"Certainly. Moses was led by God to turn over the leadership of the Israelites to Joshua. The Lord provided one miracle after another according to Joshua's great faith: the Jordan river parted so the people could cross, the walls of Jericho came tumbling down as they marched around, the sun and moon stood still in the valley of Ajalon so God could give His fighting warriors victory over their enemies.

"I treasure the promise God gave to Joshua when he was beginning his leadership: '...as I was with Moses, so I will be with thee: I will not fail thee, nor forsake thee. Be strong and of a good courage...' The Lord did exactly as He promised. He is the same today and we can claim this same promise. It makes my heart want to sing for joy!"

Abby smiled in agreement and so did the others, except Lisa. Her thoughts were elsewhere. She said, "I may have forgiven those wicked men but I cannot forget that horrible experience. I'm not yet ready to sing about it. That's asking too much. Maybe it just takes time. Or perhaps I will never forget. After all, I'm human. I still feel nauseated from being robbed like that. And my head aches. It's a shattering experience."

"We understand, Lisa." Abby's voice was soft with genuine sympathy.

Ein Karim

They turned off the main road and drove along a little-used track surrounded by fields. From the van they picked their way through overgrown grass and weeds to a stone wall. Inside the enclosure was a burial tomb of stones. "I know this is not spectacular," Abby confessed, "but Joshua was such a brave character I think we need to be reminded of his faith and how God used him. I anticipate the pleasure of meeting and talking with him someday in Heaven.

"We'll go on for a late lunch in the home of friends of mine. Israeli tractors have bulldozed some of their village walls and homes as punishment for fighting. But the people display fortitude and the church is filled with faithful Arab believers.

"You'll be surprised to find that originally this family lived in a large cave. Subsequently, they built and moved into a roomier place beside it. But we'll have the privilege of eating right in that cave. I think you'll enjoy the experience."

They did, and thanked the gentle host and hostess for a splendid meal.

After traditional coffee, they read a few verses of Scripture, sang a hymn and prayed. Again, Megan said she hated to leave this personal interaction with Arab Christians. "I love this precious fellowship with believers from another culture. It's a little taste of what heaven may be like."

Back at the guest home, Julia met them at the door and said, "Guess what! The police chief phoned and asked for Lisa. She is to go to the station as soon as possible."

"Peter, please come with me," Lisa begged.

"Abby must go with us to speak in Arabic, especially if there are any negotiations to be made," he answered.

The three of them left immediately. As soon as they walked into the station, the officer in charge went to a drawer, pulled out a blue wallet and handed it to Lisa. "Check to see if everything is there," he ordered.

She looked it over, carefully and thoroughly. "It is," she smiled and her eyes lit with pleasure. "Everything is here."

Comforting Arms

Abby thanked the chief profusely and they left.

"I cannot believe it. How in the world could this have happened?" Lisa asked excitedly as they walked back to the van.

"Is all of your money there?" asked Peter.

"Yes. I counted it twice. Even the pictures and ID, credit cards, too. Everything. Nothing is missing."

"We prayed, Lisa. And you forgave. This is God's way of showing you His power on your behalf," Peter said.

"This really is a miracle," exclaimed Abby. "My friends have told me that no one ever gets back his money or ID and especially his credit cards after his wallet has been stolen. We should have a time of thanksgiving in devotions tonight, eh, Peter?"

"That we should." And they did. Even Lisa joined in. She seemed subdued and less critical of every move Abby made.

Maybe this incident of the stolen wallet has opened Lisa's eyes to what God can do when we pray and ask His help, thought Abby.

"Before we part tonight, would you mind telling us more of the experiences you had when you lived here, Abby? Perhaps something you valued was lost or stolen?" Andrew suggested.

"Yes. That's true. Several times. We had driven to Galilee to baptize two friends in the Jordan River. We parked in a banana plantation and walked to a spot that looked negotiable. In those days, there was no official baptismal area like we saw when we visited there. The Jordan looked calm enough and my husband gingerly stepped into the water. He said later that the strong current of the river nearly swept him off his feet, and he had to hold onto the young couple tightly so they wouldn't be carried away.

"It was a happy occasion, and we were celebrating until we got back to the car. We found it unlocked and wondered why. When we opened the doors, we discovered we'd been robbed. John had left his valuables there. His keys,

Ein Karim

passport, billfold and money were all missing. What a shock that was! We went to the police but they said since we were from Jerusalem, we should report it there. Nothing was ever returned.

"Twice our car was broken into and our cameras were stolen. After I returned as a widow, I lived for a few months in Jerusalem in the home of missionaries on furlough. One day I was asked to baby-sit for friends. As soon as I got there, the phone rang. It was my neighbor. He said, 'Madam, you should come back at once. Your front door is wide open!'

"I hurried home and found the screen door unfastened and the main door taken off its hinges. Thieves had ransacked the whole house. The contents of the dresser and desk drawers were turned upside down in piles. Clothes and papers were scattered on the bed and floor. All of my jewelry and the whole month's pay were missing.

"I wedged a long pole against the screen, and the neighbor put the main door back in its place so I could lock it."

"Are you saying that you slept there that night?" asked Lisa. "How could you do such a thing? I would be scared to death."

"I think the Lord provides the courage and strength we need for every situation we encounter, if we depend upon Him."

"You can say that if you like. I know I could never endure such a life. That's enough for tonight. I'm going for a walk. Peter, will you come with me?"

"Of course, Lisa."

The couples went to their rooms. Abby watched Peter and Lisa leave. Her heart was heavy. *Oh Lord, help me not to be jealous. I admit I am. I try not to be. I know I must commit Peter into Your hands. That is the only way I can ever have peace. But I do love him and although I realize I may not be worthy of his love, I hate to see him getting involved with a woman who is not a dedicated Christian like he is. Help Lisa*

175

to change. I think she may be showing signs of softening since the wallet incident. Give her understanding so that she may be willing to commit herself and all she is to You.

Abby returned to her room reluctantly. She knew sleep would not come so she tried to read but the words looked blurred through her tears. *I know I'm feeling sorry for myself. Peter and I have had good conversations but perhaps that's all there is going to be for me.* She stared out the window, unseeing, until a couple emerged from the shadow of the home and sat down on a bench in the garden.

"Peter, let's sit here in the moonlight and talk," Lisa said. "It's time for you to tell me how you feel."

"What do you mean, Lisa?"

"Must I say more? You know very well what I mean."

"Perhaps you've misunderstood. I've tried to help you whenever you've needed it, just as I'd help anyone in need. But..."

"Oh? You haven't given me that impression."

"Then I'm truly sorry. Please forgive me."

"Well, you're making a big mistake. You'll be sorry, I assure you." Lisa's voice quivered. "Please, Peter, think about this. I have plenty of money. I need you. I want to be a better Christian. Only you can help me!" she sobbed and lifted her big blue eyes filled with tears.

Peter hesitated. *I do feel sorry for the woman. She does need help. Am I the one to continue pointing out to her the joy of living for Jesus, instead of always thinking of pleasing herself? She accuses Abby of being selfish when she's the one who's guilty! Should I be the one to guide her into a commitment of her selfishness to Christ? This is what she needs. If only I could make her understand what it means to dedicate her life to Him. Lord, is this the woman You have brought into my life so that I may teach her the meaning of the deep Spirit-filled life? I need Your guidance. I don't want to make a mistake. I had hoped You had chosen Abby for me.*

She is my ideal: a gentle, gracious, loving woman. Is she my own choice, my own desire?

"Lisa, I need time to think. Let's not talk about this again until I am ready. Now go to bed and get a good night's sleep."

"Oh, Peter, you will think seriously about this, won't you? I can't stand suspense. Please let me know soon." She smiled through her tears, knowing how attractive a woman looks to a man when she does that.

"Lisa, I need to pray before I can make any decision like this. Now let's go in. Good night."

From her window, Abby saw Peter rise abruptly and begin walking toward the veranda of the guest home. Lisa hurried to catch up, grabbed his arms and when he hesitated, hugged and kissed him. Abby turned away. She had not heard their conversation but she saw enough to think that Peter and Lisa had made a definite commitment.

"Please, Lisa. You're embarrassing yourself and me. Good night." Peter untangled his arms and quickly left her.

In his room, Peter fell on his knees at his bedside. *Oh God, show me clearly Your will. That is all I ask and want. Your Holy Spirit is my Guide. I need direction in this decision. Help me!*

Quietly an inner voice, that of the Holy Spirit dwelling within his heart, answered, *Abby is for you.*

Thank You, Father. That is all I need to know. Peter's heart leaped for joy!

Chapter 23

Bethany and the Mount of Olives

Abby said, "We're on our way to a suburb of Jerusalem where Jesus performed a special miracle. He had dear friends He loved very much. They loved Him, too. He often visited them when He was in Jerusalem. There were two sisters and a brother..."

"Mary, Martha and Lazarus in Bethany!" Megan said. "Our children love that story. The brother got sick and the sisters sent a messenger asking Jesus to come right away. But He didn't come and Lazarus died. When Jesus finally got to their village, Martha went to meet Him and said, 'Lord, if only you had come sooner my brother would not have died.'"

"Yes. Sometimes I find myself asking God why He didn't do something sooner. Then I remember this story. Jesus had a reason for the delay," Abby said.

A short distance beyond the Mount of Olives, they curved around and up to the little town of Bethany. Beside the road was a small doorway cut out of stone. Abby pointed to it and said, "There we'll find Lazarus' tomb."

"It looks dark and scary," Lisa said as they approached. "Peter, please help me." As usual, he went to her rescue. The others were not surprised. By now they were used to tolerating Lisa's obvious designs with patience. They climbed down narrow stone steps. Only a small dim light bulb hanging from the ceiling showed the way.

They were in a deep cave. Beside the steps were oblong empty beds hollowed out of stone. Some looked larger than others.

"What are these?" asked Megan "Oh, they're like the catacombs in Rome."

"Yes, empty graves," Abby answered.

"Ugh. How revolting," Lisa commented.

"Why are there so many?" asked Cindy.

"In those days they had family tombs. The small places were for children and the larger ones for adults," Abby answered softly.

"Just think, Lazarus was here four days until Jesus called him by his name and told him to come out. What a wonderful surprise that was for the family, and for all the people who had come to the funeral," Peter said. "Do you know why Jesus did not go to the sisters right away?"

"Why?" asked Megan.

"Because He said this miracle was to be for the glory of God. He could have healed Lazarus when he was sick. But to raise him from the dead was an even greater miracle. It brought more glory to God and proved His power over life and death."

"Now I understand the story a lot better," murmured Colin as they climbed back up the steps. Coming out into the sunlight, he spied a little shop across the road and went to investigate. "Oh, look! Here are slingshots! Just like you promised, Abby. Now I can get one for my son, and Peter will have one for his five stones from David's brook."

Megan joined him. "It's made of woven yarn in different colors and it looks just like the ones we've seen shepherd boys using. Won't little Joe love this one!"

"Next we'll go to the Garden of Gethsemane, where Jesus prayed before the Roman soldiers came to arrest Him." Sam drove back along the curving road. "It's on the Mount of Olives."

Through a gate they entered an olive grove. Red and yellow flowering plants and bushes bordered the neat paths.

"That tree is said to be from the roots of one that lived two thousand years ago," explained an official guide. "Others are younger. If you go into the church you'll see a big stone where Jesus might have knelt when He prayed while His disciples slept. This is where Judas brought the soldiers to arrest Him."

In the church the guests sat down to solemnly meditate about what happened there. Abby passed around the New Testament she had marked so each one could read. "And he went a little further, and fell on his face, and prayed, saying, 'O my Father, if it be possible, let this cup pass from me: nevertheless not as I will, but as thou wilt.'"

They quietly left the ancient garden and followed the narrow road where Jesus had ridden the donkey on Palm Sunday.

Abby led the group through an opening in a stone fence. The old walled city of Jerusalem was directly opposite them across the Kidron Valley. Above the stone walls, the gold Dome of the Rock glistened in the sun.

The group sat down on rocks among the olive trees. Sheep huddled nearby.

"Do you know what the Arabs call these tiny red blossoms at our feet? The 'blood-drops of Jesus.' The Bible says that when Jesus prayed, His sweat was like great drops of blood falling down to the ground. These little flowers remind us of His suffering."

Lisa was quiet. Her usual bitter retort stuck in her throat. She motioned for Peter to help her up from the rock and stayed close to him as they returned to the van. Sam took them to the Old City of Jerusalem and they entered the Christian Quarter through St. Stephen's Gate.

"We're going into the Church of St. Anne. It dates from the time of the Crusades and it's said to be the site of the home of Joachim and Anne, parents of the Virgin Mary. In the courtyard is the Pool of Bethesda. You know the story of how Jesus healed the man who had been infirm for thirty-eight years. Another grand miracle to remember," Abby said. "Here is the pool."

Cindy leaned down to dip her hand into the water. "I'm awed by this, Abby. You'll never know how much it means to us. We cannot thank you enough for taking us to these significant places."

"I suppose you realize it's lunch time?" Lisa suggested.

"You're quite right. We'll have lunch at my friend's little falafel shop and then go on."

After a tasty sandwich and cool drink they continued their tour in the Old City.

"These cobblestone streets are hard to walk on," Lisa complained, "and they're packed with tourists. I'm extremely uncomfortable. Why are we here?"

"It's Good Friday, you know. The crowds of people are following that man carrying a large wooden cross."

"That must be like the one Jesus carried and it looks heavy!" remarked Colin. "Where's he taking it?" he asked as he panned the scene.

"Along the same route that Jesus carried His, called the Via Dolorosa, the way of sadness or suffering. Let's walk along and I'll point out the eight Stations of the Cross that devout people visit every year in remembrance of this special day. First is the Praetorium, Pilate's Judgment Hall where Jesus was sentenced to be crucified. Now it is a Muslim school.

"The Second is the Church of Flagellation and a Chapel of Scourging where Jesus was tortured and given a crown of thorns to wear. Farther along we see an arch where Pilate is said to have spoken with Jesus, and beyond is a chapel called the Prison of Christ.

"The Third Station is a small museum we'll pass, and the Fourth is where Jesus met his Mother. A Catholic church marks the place and a crypt shows a mosaic in the form of a pair of sandals at the spot where Mary stood.

"We're coming to the Fifth, a small chapel where Simon the Cyrenian is said to have taken Jesus' cross to bear. The Sixth is the house of St. Veronica who supposedly wiped the sweat and blood from Jesus' face and the imprint of his features remained on the cloth she used.

"Now we've come out into the main market. Opposite us is the Seventh Station, marking the Gate of Judgment through which Jesus passed as he left Jerusalem. The Eighth Station is where Jesus spoke with the women who followed, telling them not to weep for him but for their children."

"Well, let's get out of here. I'm being pushed and pulled about in this crowd and I don't like it," Lisa grumped.

Abby made no reply. They had finished all she had planned for the day and she was already leading them toward Jaffa Gate where Sam met them.

That evening in the dining room Julia served traditional Arab sweet cakes. They were lavishly sprinkled with powdered sugar, and with coffee they made a delectable dessert. "Sam's wife made these," she said. "The rings like a small doughnut are stuffed with mashed spiced dates. They represent Jesus' crown of thorns. These round ones are filled with nuts, cinnamon and sugar. They are supposed to be the stones people threw at Jesus."

"Here's Sam," said Julia. "Please thank your wife for making the cakes."

"Would you like to come to my house and meet my family?"

"Thank you, we'd be happy to do that if it's alright with Julia," answered Abby.

Everyone except Lisa tramped along a narrow path through the woods and stopped in front of a small stone house. Sam pointed to his trees. "These are fig, and those are apricot. Beyond are almond and apple. In back is the vegetable garden."

A long trellis of grapevines arched the path to the front door. Bright red geraniums blossomed in the window-boxes. Sam's mother graciously welcomed the guests and showed them into the living room. It was tastefully furnished with a comfortable sofa, chairs, coffee tables, colorful carpet and drapes.

"This looks like home," remarked Megan. "There's even a TV."

A little boy shyly entered the room. Sam took his hand and said, "This is my son. His name is Nimir." He smiled as the little boy ran to welcome Abby with a kiss and hug.

"Do you know what my name means? Aunty Abby, don't tell, please," the boy said with a chuckle. "Grrrrr! Grrrrr!" He showed his teeth menacingly and made his hands look like claws ready to scratch.

Colin ventured a guess. "A cat?"

"No."

"A lion?" Megan grinned.

"No!"

"A tiger?" Andrew played along.

"Yes!" Nimir and Abby laughed together.

"Come and see my rabbits," invited Nimir. He led them out behind the house.

"Oh, Easter bunnies!" exclaimed Megan. She held a small one and stroked its soft fur and long ears.

A big friendly cat appeared and rubbed Cindy's legs. She picked it up but it jumped out of her arms and ran to a box.

"She has kittens. Would you like to see them?" Nimir handed a tiny kitten to Megan and another to Colin.

"Wouldn't our children love these? One for each of them!" Megan exclaimed.

"Sam is calling us for coffee," Abby said, and they gathered to enjoy fruit, more sweet cakes and hot chocolate. Peter thanked their host and asked, "What should we say when we leave? I know you have special wishes in Arabic for different occasions."

"To be very polite, you would say, 'May God increase your wealth,'" answered Sam.

"That's unique. So be it! God bless and be with you all. May you have a very happy Easter."

When they returned to the guest home, Lisa met them. "Why didn't you wait for me? I was coming," she fumed.

Comforting Arms

"I'm sorry," Abby apologized. "I thought you had gone to your room to retire."

"This early? No way. You certainly are not looking after your responsibilities, are you? Won't you ever learn? Such thoughtlessness is inexcusable."

Lisa sounded like she was up to her old tricks. Abby felt disappointed. She had hoped the incident of the stolen wallet and Lisa's prayer to forgive the thieves had changed the woman's attitude. But she decided it was wishful thinking on her part.

"Let's all go to the lounge and have devotions," Peter suggested.

"Good idea," Andrew agreed and led the way.

After prayers, Peter asked, "What impressed you most about this day?"

Without hesitating, Lisa began. "It's been nothing but sickness and death. First Lazarus, then Gethsemane and the 'way of the cross' or whatever it's called. I came on this tour to forget trouble and suffering and that's all we've seen and talked about all day!"

"It is a part of life, you can't deny that," Andrew said. "I've seen a lot of it in my work."

"Well, I want to ignore it and have a good time. We live here and now. Why worry about tomorrow? Good night, all," she announced and flounced out of the room without a backward glance.

What? No evening stroll with Peter? Abby was surprised. Her musing was interrupted by Peter's voice. "Tell me, Abby, what are your plans for the future?" He motioned for her to sit beside him on the sofa. The two couples and Julia discreetly left the room.

"After this furlough I probably will return to continue working here. I'm not ready to retire yet. I've been asked by a publisher to write my experiences in a book. When that is finished, and eventually after I'm retired, I may apply to go on short-term missions."

"What kind of work would you do, and where would you go?"

"I might teach child evangelism, English, Christian education or history of missions in a Bible college. I would go wherever missionaries need someone to help."

"No grass will grow under your feet, Abby. I admire you for wanting to continue serving the Lord."

"Someone said, 'A woman is like a Cadillac. She doesn't really get going until she hits seventy!' But it's too soon to think about that yet. As the Lord directs. I want to be in the center of His will, always."

"Have you ever thought of marrying again?"

"Yes. But only if it were for love and if I felt assured that it was definitely God's plan."

"I agree on both counts. And like you, I want to continue doing whatever our Lord wants me to do as long as I can. I've begun writing a teacher's manual on Biblical missions."

"I'm glad to hear that. Anything that promotes missions has my approval and is close to my heart."

"We see eye to eye on these things, don't we?"

"Yes, Peter, we do."

He stood up, took both her hands in his and held them gently, then leaned over and placed a light kiss on her forehead. "Good night, Abby dear. Happy dreams."

"And to you," she answered, her voice trembling.

Chapter 24

Easter

The wind tugged at Abby's jacket and she wrapped it around snugly, fastening the zipper. "These Judean mountains are chilly early in the morning, aren't they?"

"I'd like to know why in the world we need to be up at this ungodly hour," grumbled Lisa. "It's cold and I'm sleepy. I don't like this at all."

Abby had warned her friends that they would need to be ready early on Sunday morning because there might be standing room only for the six o'clock sunrise service at the Garden Tomb. Visitors from all over the world would be gathering there to celebrate Easter.

She had awakened everyone at five o'clock so they could leave the guest home in plenty of time. There was not much traffic on the road to Jerusalem, and they arrived as people were beginning to line up in front of the closed doors.

"Listen, some Japanese are speaking in their own language," Cindy said.

"How do you know they're Japanese? They might be Chinese or Korean," Lisa argued.

"I have some Japanese friends at home and I've heard them speak many times. They've taught me a few words. And listen to that English accent. It's not British and it's not Welsh, is it, Peter? Where are those people from?"

"They're Australian. Not far behind us are Africans in their native dress. I think they might be from Kenya. It sounds like they're speaking Swahili. I learned a bit of it

Easter

from one of my students. That language is really different, isn't it!"

"I'll say it is," agreed Megan. "Could I ever learn to speak that? We've met a lot of Arabs and I've picked up some words. It's fun trying to make all those sounds in my throat."

"Look, they're opening the doors. Here we go."

"Listen to that organ playing." Cindy was pleased. "And see these gorgeous deep scarlet hibiscus blooms and those exquisite flowering plants. This really is a garden!"

"There's a holy hush in this place. And down there must be the tomb. It looks like a cave with a door. Can we go in?" Megan asked.

"Yes," Abby nodded, "we're early so we can see it before the service starts. But first, let's follow these signs pointing to Calvary."

They hurried along a path leading past more shrubs and flowers, and came to a platform. "Step up here," Abby said as she pointed to the opposite hill. "Do you see those two huge gouges in the dirt and stones, and below them an indentation that looks like a nose? That is Golgotha, 'The place of the skull.' And above, at the top of the hill, is Calvary. It's still a place of death because now it's a Muslim cemetery."

"It hurts me to think Jesus had to die when He was perfectly sinless," Megan said.

"He did it for us--for the whole world--but the wonderful part is coming next. Let's go and see the tomb."

They climbed down steps to a stone wall and entered through a small door. Inside was a cave with empty tombs hollowed out of the limestone rock.

"I'm awed by this inspiring proof of the resurrection," Colin said. "And look at this sign over the door: He is risen; He is not here."

"This is the heart of Christianity," Peter murmured.

Lisa, to everyone's surprise, was silent as they moved away quietly so that other people could have a turn.

Abby found a bench with space enough for them all to sit together. "We can gaze at the open door of the tomb and meditate as we listen to the music."

It was cold sitting outside, but their hearts were warm with joy as they joined hundreds of people singing, "He Arose" and "He Lives." Tears ran down Cindy's cheeks. Andrew knew she was weeping with happiness. She had wanted to see this place more than any other in the Holy Land. Like Peter, she had often remarked, "The cross and the resurrection of Jesus are the heart of our Christian message!"

During the service, a woman sang a special number with meaningful words:

>"I stood before the Garden Tomb
>   where Christ lay long ago,
>And weeping followers came to mourn
>   the One Who loved them so.
>But look, that grave's an empty bed!
>   He's risen as He said,
>And living in Heaven's glory
>   to reign for all eternity,
>Where I shall share a part.
>   I know today that Jesus lives,
>For He lives in my heart!"

Following the service, Abby took her friends to a restaurant for breakfast. Then they walked a short distance to the Old City of Jerusalem. Broad stone steps led down to Damascus Gate. Along the narrow streets, merchants were selling clothes, shoes, toys, vegetables, fruit, bread, eggs, nuts and sweets.

"I see they use moneychangers here," remarked Colin as he read a sign over a small doorway. "I've been using dollars. Aren't there any banks?"

"The Arabs prefer to use a man who will take your check and give you Israeli shekels in exchange. He's the banker. Usually his rate of exchange is higher than the bank would pay. This way, both parties profit."

"Look out!" Andrew shouted as a donkey carrying milk cans trotted down the narrow street. He bumped Megan and she giggled, then burst into peals of laughter. Before she could stop, along came a fat lady with a big basket of cabbages on her head. She was bulldozing her way through the crowd and rudely jabbed her elbow into Lisa's side, knocking her off balance. Andrew caught her before she fell.

Megan could not control her laughter and they all wanted to join in, but the insulted look on Lisa's face prohibited merriment. She gritted her teeth, narrowed her eyes and turned to look daggers at the lady's back.

Colin stopped to watch a group of boys huddled together on the sidewalk. "I wonder what they're doing," he said as he edged closer. "Oh, they're shooting marbles just like we do. Good game, fellows!" he commented.

Farther along more boys were playing with hard-boiled colored eggs. Abby explained the rules. "One boy tries to smash the other's egg by holding his own in his closed fist with just enough of the egg showing top and bottom to hit or be hit. Whoever succeeds in smashing the other's egg is the winner."

"Fun," thought Colin. "Our family must try that."

They met a man balancing a big tray of buns on his head. He offered to sell one to each of them. Every bun had a red colored egg baked into the center. Andrew decided he was not hungry enough to try one. Lisa turned away, grunting, "Ugh, how sickening."

A little girl approached carrying a palm branch with fresh flowers--roses, carnations and daisies--tucked into the woven pockets of the fronds. She happily posed for Colin to take her picture.

"She's on her way to church," Abby explained as several more children came along carrying flowers. They were dressed in their best clothes. The boys wore shirts and ties and the girls, in colorful fancy dresses, chattered excitedly when they saw the video camera.

"We're following the Via Dolorosa again. We were here on Good Friday."

"Yes, I remember," Lisa said. "It's nothing but up or down. This Old City is all hills."

"Oh, what's that thing coming along?" Megan asked. "It looks like a miniature tractor pulling a trailer."

"That's a garbage pick-up. The streets are too narrow for cars or trucks to negotiate."

"Must we climb up, up, up all these steps? I'm out of breath," Lisa complained. "Slow down Peter."

"We're nearly there. Only a few more until we arrive at the church," Abby said.

"More steps yet?" Lisa was disgusted. "Where is the place? You're punishing us, Abby. Peter, help me."

"Here we are."

The glass windows of the church were painted artistically with stalks of wheat, pomegranates, grapes, olives and figs. "How very beautiful and appropriate!" exclaimed Cindy.

A smiling young man welcomed them and gave Abby a big hug. She introduced her friends as he showed them to a seat.

"My name is Johnny," he said. "If you need anything, I'll be happy to help you. Abby can translate the Arabic into English for you."

"Doesn't this music remind you of our visit on Mt. Carmel and the wonderful songfest at the hotel?" Andrew whispered to Cindy.

The minister greeted everyone with the words, "Christ arose!" and the congregation answered, "Truly He arose!"

Abby explained the gist of the sermon. "Because Jesus lives, we should live to show people what He is like. He is our example. We are to be like Him."

After the meeting, several young girls served everyone coffee, colored eggs and sweet cakes.

"These are like the ones we had at Sam's house," Cindy said. "Mmm, delicious!"

As they were leaving, Johnny said, "Go in peace. God be with you."

"What an inspiring way to celebrate Easter!" exclaimed Megan as they threaded their way through the market.

"I love it," agreed Cindy. "It's so meaningful and full of precious memories."

They tramped along a level street where only a few shops were open. Most of them were closed, signifying that the merchants were Christians and had gone to church. Lisa balked at the sight of more steps to climb.

"Lisa, these are the last steps we'll have to negotiate. We're to meet the van outside Jaffa Gate. It's more convenient. We'll drive on to Bethlehem for dinner in a small, private hotel room. Julia will meet us there. She's already ordered a famous Jordanian dish for us."

The waiter was a personal friend of Abby's. At her request, he had arranged for them to sit on rugs on the floor. He and a helper carried in a giant-size round tray of rice and lamb and urged them to gather around it and eat with their fingers, Bedouin style. With Abby as their example, Colin and Megan immediately tried and liked it. "It tastes better, eating this way, really it does! Try it," Megan urged the others.

Her enthusiasm was inspiring. Cindy and Andrew began hesitantly. Lisa frowned disdainfully and refused. "Far too messy for my taste!" The waiter quietly handed her a spoon and a separate plate.

It was tricky to get the food from hand to mouth without spilling some. Peter and Julia joined in the fun and soon they were laughing at their own clumsiness.

That night Julia arranged a weenie roast for her guests. Sam had a snapping bonfire going in the field, with stone benches in a half-circle around it. His wife helped serve hot cocoa and cookies.

After they sang a few choruses accompanied by Sam on the accordion, Abby said, "This is our last night. Tell us what has impressed you about the things we've seen, or about life here in the Holy Land."

"Our last night? Oh no! The time has gone too quickly. It's been a great new exciting experience. Isn't there more to see?" asked Megan. "I've learned so much I wouldn't know where to begin. I loved Bethlehem most of all, I think. But it's hard to decide."

"Yes, there are many more places to visit. But we've completed our schedule for this time. Perhaps someday you can return."

"Well," began Colin, "I've been impressed with the way stones are cut for building purposes, and the size of Jericho's walls. What a miracle that was. Solomon's Pools were quite an engineering feat, too!"

Andrew said, "I appreciated seeing the places where Jesus healed the sick. It made me think about His great love and compassion for suffering humanity."

"One of my favorite places was Mt. Carmel and the meaningful singing of the Arab Christians at the conference center," added Cindy.

"Thank you, Abby, for taking us on one adventure after another," Peter said. "We've stored up a treasure-chest of unique memories. I especially loved the trip to Galilee and seeing all the places where Jesus performed miracles. It has encouraged me to believe that since Jesus is the same 'yesterday, today and forever,' He still does miracles for us today."

After a lengthy pause, Lisa spoke up. "All right. Now it's my turn to admit that I think a miracle has happened to me. After being with you and observing your Christ-likeness and tactfulness in not pushing but only trying to help, I..."

She hesitated and bowed her head. "And after the sermon in church this morning about living for Jesus, I prayed a long time this afternoon and finally surrendered myself and all my desires to Christ. I feel like a new person. I know it may take time to get rid of my habit of criticizing, complaining, grumbling, selfishness and an unforgiving spirit, but with God's help I'm determined to change and be more like He wants me to be. And I'm extremely sorry for the way I've behaved, especially to you, Abby. Please forgive me."

"Oh, Lisa, I'm so glad for you!" Abby spontaneously gave her a big hug.

"We all are, Lisa," Peter added as he shook her hand. "Congratulations on taking that step of faith."

Lisa held tightly to Peter's hand and said, "Listen, everyone. Congratulations may be in order. As you know, Peter and I have become close friends. Shall we make the announcement now?" She sounded determined to have her own way.

Abby did not wait to hear more. She quietly slipped away, unnoticed. *O Lord, help me!* she prayed as she hurried to her room. Once again she fell to her knees. *Lord, I turn this problem over to You. Take my desires. I place them in Your hands. I submit to Your will.* Slowly, the soothing, sweet, comforting peace of the Lord enveloped her. *Thank You, Father, for restoring to me the 'contentment of commitment.'* At last, her heart was at rest.

At the bonfire, Andrew looked from Lisa to Peter, surprised and puzzled. "Is this true, then?"

"Yes!" Lisa answered quickly, before Peter could answer. "We…"

"No, not at all," Peter interrupted before she could continue. He drew a deep breath. "Lisa, you had no right to assume that I would agree with your announcement. You did not ask for my approval before you spoke. I would have told you that I've prayed for God's guidance and I do not believe this is His plan for you or for me. I'm sorry if you're hurt by my decision, but you did not wait for me to explain. I'm also sorry you have misunderstood my motives. Please forgive me. I've only been trying to help you as any Christian man would do under the circumstances."

"Come, Lisa, let's forget this ever happened," Cindy urged, and taking her by the hand, led her away from the bonfire.

"I've never been so humiliated in all my life! How could you embarrass me like this?" she flung back at Peter as she stumbled along the path. It didn't occur to her that her actions were purely selfish, based upon her own desires, without considering Peter's. "Now I hate that man," she stormed furiously.

"You don't mean that," Cindy chided. "After the way you talked about giving yourself to Christ? You did make that decision, didn't you?"

Lisa stopped short, considering. "Yes. You're right. I did. I just forgot. I guess that old way of doing things selfishly and responding angrily if I don't get my own way has to be changed. Thanks, Cindy, for reminding me."

The two women were surprised to see a visitor in the lounge. Lisa's face turned a ghastly white as she gasped, "Harold! What are you doing here?" Instantly remembering her manners, she introduced the tall, good-looking man to Cindy.

"Meet my husband, Harold. We've been separated, as you know."

He acknowledged the introduction politely and turned to Lisa. "I came to find you. I can't live without you, Lisa. I've been miserable ever since I left you. Please forgive me. I've always loved you. Let's renew our marriage vows."

"I...don't know what to say. We'll have to talk this over. I've just committed my life to Christ and from now on, I'm changing drastically."

"I've done the same thing. I guess God had to bring us to this place before we could consider facing life together again. With Him in control, our marriage will be totally different."

Easter

"Yes. You're right. I think I've been trying to dodge the fact that I've always loved you, too. Now that I've asked God to forgive my sins, I know turn-about is fair play, so it means I should forgive you and ask you to forgive me."

"Done! Is there a minister around? This would be a good place to start over."

"Not so fast! Let's go back home together and take it from there."

Cindy withdrew quietly, thinking what a grand climax this was for the tour. God certainly answered our prayers. I never thought it would happen so soon!

Peter watched the flames of the bonfire slowly die down and breathed a sigh of relief. Andrew, Megan and Colin smiled sympathetically and quietly walked away, leaving him alone. Immediately he knew what he wanted to do. Now was the time to confirm his relationship with Abby. He carefully scanned the paths but could not find her. She was not in the lounge. In desperation, he knocked on her door.

Abby quickly brushed away her tears, opened the door, and was shocked to see Peter. "We need to talk, Abby. Please come with me."

"Of course," she answered cheerfully, and wondered why Lisa was not with him.

He led her outside to a stone bench beneath the rose arbor. Moonlight shone on her wavy hair, and her big brown eyes sparkled. She looked more beautiful than ever to him.

Without hesitating he said, "I don't know how much you heard of the conversation between Lisa and myself. I regret that she completely misunderstood my motives in helping her. There was no announcement. I made that very clear.

"I've learned to love you very much, Abby. I believe the Lord brought me here to find you. Do you think you could ever love me?"

Abby slowly responded, "Yes...I do love you, Peter."

"That's what I wanted to know. Now I can ask...would you do me the honor of becoming my wife?"

"I...would be happy to marry you."

He gathered her in his arms and as she rested her head on his chest, she felt supreme, overwhelming joy. This was "the contentment of commitment." At last comforting arms were holding her. Her heart said, *Thank You, Father, for Your gracious gift of this love. I cherish it.*

Peter bent and sealed their love with light, gentle kisses like the soft brush of butterfly wings on her forehead, eyes, cheeks, nose and chin, then a long, tender sweet kiss on her lips. He murmured, "Heavenly Father, thank You for bringing us together and giving us this privilege of loving and caring for each other. May we serve You together for Your glory. Amen."

Bibliography

Roget's Thesaurus, Cardinal Edition, Pocket Books, Inc., NY, NY

A Complete Concordance to the Holy Scriptures, Alexander Cruden

Unger's Bible Dictionary, Merle Unger, Moody Press, 1966, Chicago IL, Fleming H Revell Co., Chicago IL

This is Israel, Sylvia Mann Palphot LTD, Herzlia, IsraelnHai-Bar Wildlife Reserve, Israel - picture folder

Amir's Pictorial Maps, Fellowship Tours, Inc., Phoenix, AZ

Israel Guide, Zev Vilnay, Hamakor Press, Jerusalem, Israel The Land of the Bible, map, Shlomo Hizak, Jerusalem, Israel

Berllitz Travel Guide, Editions Berlitz, Lausanne, Switzerland

The Negev and Sinai, Rinna Samuel, Weidenfeld and Nicolson, Japhet Press, Tel Aviv, Israel